Dog Bones and Dead Bodies

Pupcakes and Peril

Paige Tyler

Copyright © 2025 by Paige Tyler

All rights reserved.

No part of this publication may be reproduced, distributed, or transmitted in any form or by any means, including photocopying, recording, or other electronic or mechanical methods, without the prior written permission of the publisher, except as permitted by U.S. copyright law. For permission requests, contact [include publisher/author contact info].

The story, all names, characters, and incidents portrayed in this production are fictitious. No identification with actual persons (living or deceased), places, buildings, and products is intended or should be inferred.

Cover Image by Anastasia

Editing by Jennifer Jakes/The Killion Group

Proofreading by RVP

With special thanks to my extremely patient and understanding husband, without whose help and support I couldn't have pursued my dream job of becoming a writer. You're my sounding board, my idea man, my critique partner, and the absolute best research assistant any girl could ask for!
Thank you!

Chapter 1

"You know those are dog treats, right?"

From where she stood over by the long rustic-looking table with its plethora of three-tiered stands piled high with a variety of homemade dog treats, Lucy Shaw glanced up from the peanut butter bone-shaped cookie she was snacking on, blue eyes twinkling. "I know, but I'm hungry and these taste delicious. Besides, I'm eating for two."

Tassie Drake let out a snort of laughter as Lucy went back to nibbling. She and Lucy had been best friends since high school, so Tassie knew all her weird habits, but this was a new one. And while Tassie and her sister, Abby, made all the cookies at Pupcakes, the doggy bakery they co-owned, with ingredients you could certainly eat, sugar wasn't one of them, which meant they didn't taste delicious at all.

Unless you were a dog, of course.

Beside Tassie, her adorable Chiweenie, Baxter, regarded her from where he sat on his fluffy round donut bed on the floor. Black with some caramel, he had a patch of white right on his chin that made it look like he was smiling whenever he looked up at you. Right now, it made Tassie think he found the idea of Lucy snacking on those peanut butter treats quite amusing.

From over in the open kitchen where Abby was rolling out a fresh batch of dog cookies on the big wood counter, Tassie saw her sister shake her head, light brown ponytail swinging from side to side as she tried not to laugh.

But like Lucy said, she was eating for two. And she *had* been craving some very weird foods now that she was in her second trimester. Petite with shoulder-length dark curly hair, she was the definition of glowing. After stuffing a few more treats in the clear plastic bag—for her dog this time—she closed it with a twist-tie, then walked over to the counter where Tassie waited.

"Henry's replacement arrived today," Lucy said conversationally as she pulled out her credit card.

The town's one and only police detective, Henry Olson, had recently retired after three decades of dedicated service. After living in Bluewater Bay their whole lives, he and his wife decided to move to Florida to be closer to their children and grandchildren. Everyone thought the department would promote one of their four officers, but instead, they'd hired someone from the outside.

Tassie rang up the price of the dog treats, giving her the usual first responder discount because she was the daytime dispatcher with the police department. "Oh, yeah? Is he nice?"

"Seems to be." Lucy glanced at her as she tapped her card against the reader. "Cute, too. I could introduce you if you want."

Tassie purposely ignored her sister who was listening to the conversation about her love life with way too much interest and gave Lucy a pointed look. "The last time you introduced me to someone, he told me I looked like a younger version of his mother."

"Eww. Really?" She made a face. "All the more reason to let me introduce you to Jack. So you can forget about that disaster."

Tassie opened her mouth, but Lucy didn't even stop for breath.

"Before you ask, Jack Sterling is twenty-eight and originally from Albany, New York, where he's been a detective for the past five years. He isn't married—obviously. *And* he has a dog."

Okay, having a dog was definitely a plus, but still.

"I wasn't going to ask," Tassie said. "Besides, why is everybody so interested in setting me up with someone? I already have a man in my life—Baxter. He never hogs the remote or complains about what I watch on TV. He never cares that I take all the blankets at night. He never offers unsolicited advice. And I never have to worry that he's cheating on me with the waitress at the local grill and bar."

Her friend frowned. "That last part was oddly specific. Not every man is a toad like the former boyfriend of yours who shall remain nameless."

Tassie knew that, of course, but that didn't keep her from being frustrated with the male gender when it came to dating.

"Hmm. I seem to remember that you introduced me to *that* toad as well," she pointed out. "You don't have a very good track record when it comes to matchmaking, you know?"

Lucy had the grace to look at least a little chagrined. "How was I supposed to know he was a serial cheater?"

Tassie just looked at her.

"Baxter is absolutely adorable and perfect in every way, I'll give you that," Lucy agreed when it was clear she wasn't going to say anything else. "But finding someone to join your little family wouldn't be a bad thing, would it?"

"No. But not everyone is as lucky as you, Lucy. You hit the jackpot with Andrew."

It was true. Lucy and her firefighter husband had met through work since the police department worked closely with fire and rescue. Handsome, outdoorsy, and laid-back, Andrew was sweet, caring, and an altogether great guy. All in all, he was the perfect match for Lucy.

"The big lug does all right," her friend said with a teasing grin. "But we're talking about you here not me."

She sighed. "And when the right guy comes along, I'll be more than happy to give him a chance."

"How will you know if a guy is the *right* guy unless you go out with him?" Lucy countered.

Tassie wished she could come up with an argument for that, but unfortunately, she was drawing a blank. It would be nice if there was some kind of computer program that'd tell you if a guy was boyfriend material or not. She flipped her long brown hair over her shoulder, then leaned her hip against the counter and folded her arms.

"How do you know so much about this new detective already anyway? I thought you said he just got here."

Lucy shrugged. "He did. I did most of my research on him before that. I like to know who I'm working with."

"You should have been a cop, you know that?" Tassie told her.

"Um, that's a hard no. I don't like the idea of getting shot at. I'll stay at my desk, thank you very much. Speaking of which, my lunch break is almost over so I'd better get back." She swung her oversized bag up on her shoulder. "By the way, Andrew is working a double, so you and Baxter want to come over for dinner tonight? I hate eating alone."

As a firefighter, Andrew sometimes worked back-to-back shifts.

Tassie glanced at Baxter to see her fur baby smiling up at her. Tassie grinned back.

"That's a yes," Tassie said to Lucy.

"Great!" She looked over at Abby. "You and Finn in, too?"

At the sound of his name, Abby's cute brown Dachshund, Finn, looked up from the stainless-steel bowl of water he had his head in.

"You know it," Abby said.

Lucy smiled. "I'll see the four of you later then. Toodles."

As she walked out of the shop, cool air swept in, making Tassie glad she and her sister had decided to locate the check-out counter toward the back of the store instead of near the front. It might say spring on the calendar, however, the state of Maine clearly didn't get the memo because it still felt like winter out there.

But she'd promised Baxter that she'd take him to the dog park that afternoon, so they'd both be venturing out into the cold. As soon as Abby got the batch of peanut butter treats she was working on in the oven so she could take over for Tassie at the counter. Which, from glancing at her sister, should be any minute now.

Graham Bartlett, another of Pupcakes regular customers, finished his shopping and walked over to set two bags of dog treats on the counter along with a box of cupcakes he'd purchased at Cozy Cupcakery, the bakery next door.

"Those look delicious," Tassie said, taking in the chocolate caramel cupcakes through the clear window on the top of the purple box. "Gwen's cupcakes are to die for, aren't they?"

He chuckled. "They are wicked good."

"Better not let your sister hear you say that," Tassie teased.

His sister, Irene, owned Dreamy Desserts, the bakery a few stores down and on the other side of the street. Even though Gwen's Cupcakery specialized in cupcakes while Dreamy Desserts made everything from cookies to pie to the most delicious, moist, decadent chocolate cake on the planet, Irene was always in competition with Gwen. It had been like that since they were kids. And now that they'd be going up against each other in a baking contest next month, their rivalry would be even more intense. Since Tassie was friends with both of them, there was no way she was getting in the middle of that battle.

Maybe they'd end up being co-champions or something. One could only hope.

Graham turned the color of his curly red hair. "Don't I know it! But I only stopped because it's a coworker's birthday and Gwen's bakery was on the way. I didn't drop by specifically to see her or anything like that."

Sitting on the floor beside her, Baxter gave Tassie the side eye. He seemed to have a knack for knowing when people were lying. And Graham was most certainly being less than truthful at the moment. Because he most certainly had a crush on Gwen Swanson. Not that he probably didn't love her cupcakes. Although, Tassie wasn't joking. He'd better not let his sister ever hear him say it.

Tassie couldn't help but smile at Graham. "Of course not. How is Charlie?"

Graham let out a sound that was somewhere between a laugh and a sigh like he was relieved to talk about something other than the pastry chef he was sweet on. "He's doing great. I installed a doggy door for him the other day, which the squirrels aren't happy about since he can now terrorize them whenever he wants."

She laughed, chatting with him about why dogs loved chasing squirrels so much as she finished ringing up his purchase.

Abby walked over as Graham left, attention focused on her cell phone and a big grin on her face. Older than Tassie's twenty-five by a couple years, Abby was the business side of the doggy bakery. In fact, it had actually been her idea to open the store. Tassie had already been making doggy cookies for Baxter and Finn as well as for dogs belonging to family and friends, so when Abby suggested starting a business a few years ago, she'd been all for it. She loved dogs and she loved baking, so it was a win-win. And in all honesty, Tassie hadn't been thrilled with her job as a pharmacy tech at the time even though her employer had been great, giving her flexible hours so she could go to college to get her degree. Classes like biology and chemistry had always been easy for her, so becoming a pharmacist seemed like a great idea, but after working as a tech, she realized it wasn't what she wanted. Luckily, her business-savvy sister had come to the rescue otherwise she'd probably be filling prescriptions right now.

"You look happy about something," Tassie remarked.

"I am," Abby said. "I just booked a therapy session for Finn with Isaac Bridger."

Tassie looked at her in surprise. "The dog psychologist who Mom and Dad were talking about the other day?"

Her sister nodded excitedly. "Yup."

Their parents had a veterinary practice in Bluewater Bay and told everyone and anyone about how remarkable Isaac was when it came to helping dogs and their owners. If Mom and Dad endorsed him, then the guy knew his stuff.

"Why would Finn need a session with a dog psychologist?" Tassie asked. "He doesn't have any behavioral issues."

"I know," Abby agreed. "But it was the best way I could think of to meet Isaac."

Ah. Now it was starting to make sense. Kind of. Though from the expression on Finn's face, he didn't seem to think much of Abby's plan.

"So he's a hunk, I take it?"

Her sister laughed. "Duh. I wouldn't be going to all this trouble if he wasn't."

Abby pulled up something on her phone, then turned it around so Tassie could see. It was a photo of the aforementioned Isaac from his Facebook page. Dark blond hair, brown eyes, and an angular jaw with a trace of stubble, he was cute. And totally her sister's type.

"Wouldn't it be easier to show up at his office and introduce yourself, then tell him that he's welcome to drop by Pupcakes anytime with some brochures or business cards?" Tassie suggested. "Almost everyone in town who has a dog comes in here."

Her sister turned her phone around to gaze at the photo on the screen. "Easier? Maybe. But then what?"

"Um, ask him out."

Tassie's own love life might be something resembling a reality TV show at the moment but that didn't mean she could give her sister advice on the subject.

Abby didn't call her on it though. But that was only because she was too busy looking at Tassie like she'd just suggested Abby jump in the bay naked—in the middle of winter.

"I can't do that!" she said. "At least not until Isaac and I get to know each other. Hence why I'm taking Finn for therapy."

"Uh-huh." Tassie folded her arms. "And don't you think that a dog psychologist as good as Isaac is going to figure out that Finn doesn't have any behavioral issues?"

Sitting on the floor beside Tassie, Baxter appeared to be as interested in the answer to that question as she was.

Before Abby could reply, the door to the bakery opened and Sara Larson rushed in, practically falling over Roxie, her Jack Russell, as she hustled her dog inside. Closing the door behind her, she smoothed her blonde bob and took a deep breath, then let it out slowly.

"Sara?" Tassie said even as Baxter pranced around the counter, tail wagging. "Are you okay?"

"What? Yes. No. I don't know." She made a face as she walked toward Tassie. "I just got into it with Conrad Meyers."

Well, that explained it. Conrad Meyers was a mean old man who wanted everyone—and their four-legged friends--to get off his lawn. Unfortunately, the town decided to put their beautiful dog park on the same street as his house, which meant every dog owner in Bluewater Bay had to walk past his property to get there.

Tassie crouched down to pet both Baxter and Roxie. "What happened?"

Sara wasn't only a regular at the bakery. She'd been a good friend since Tassie had met her a few years ago when she'd purchased some of Sara's delightful handmade soaps for Abby's birthday.

Sara sighed. "Roxie and I were walking past that creep's house when she yanked the leash out of my hand and ran across his precious lawn and into the backyard to chase a squirrel. I immediately went after her, but before I could get to her, Conrad came out of the house like he was shot out of a cannon. He shouted at me to get 'that *dog*' out of his yard and I completely lost it. I'm surprised you didn't hear us screaming all the way over here. But I couldn't help it. I've never met anyone so infuriating in my life." She joined Tassie down near the floor to run her hand over Roxie's coarse fur. "I think I scared my poor baby."

Tassie caressed Baxter's silky upright ears and gave Sara a smile. "Come on, let's get Roxie a treat so she can forget all about that nasty man."

Baxter grinned and wagged his tail wildly at the mention of a treat.

Laughing, Tassie leaned over to give him a kiss on the head and added, "Yes, you get a treat, too. Finn, as well."

As Sara filled a bag with some homemade doggy cookies, she chatted with Abby while Tassie gave Baxter, Finn, and Roxie the tiny treats she and her sister kept on top of the counter in a ceramic canister for those special pooches—which was every dog that came into the bakery, of course.

Sara and Roxie left a little later, both of them thankfully much more relaxed.

"Okay," Tassie said to her sister. "We're off to the dog park."

"Be careful," Abby said. "And don't get into any fights with Conrad. He sounds like he's more ornery than usual today."

Promising she'd be careful—and wouldn't get into a fight with Conrad—Tassie dressed Baxter in his cute little plaid fleece vest, then his harness before hooking him onto his leash. Shrugging into her coat, she put on her hat, then grabbed her crossbody bag and sunglasses. A moment later, they were heading for the door.

Chilly air coming in off the water enveloped them the moment they stepped outside, swirling Tassie's hair around her face. Thankfully, the sun more than made up for the brisk spring weather and Baxter pranced along happily beside her down the sidewalk.

Built on the bay back in the late 1700's, the town of Bluewater Bay was filled with loads of historic charm from the meticulous architecture to the hand-carved signs. Besides Pupcakes and Cozy Confections, it boasted a coffee shop, art gallery, ice cream parlor, and bookstore, as well as several clothing stores and gift shops. Bluewater Bay even had an old-fashioned general store called The General Store. Owned by a sweet older couple, it was part restaurant, part grocery, part gift shop, and served the most delicious lobster rolls anywhere—at least that's what everyone in town said. She'd have to take their word for it since she didn't eat seafood.

She waved to Gwen and the other shop owners as she and Baxter walked, stopping to chat with some of them, much to Baxter's delight. He loved people as much as he loved his fellow dogs.

Soon enough, they reached the edge of town where the shops gave way to equally charming homes. The stroll to the dog park was along a beautifully scenic path with the blue waters of the bay on the left complete with charter fishing boats, sailboats, and the occasional yacht. Sometimes, in the late spring to early fall, you could even see a cruise ship in the distance. But it was the majestic Indigo Point Lighthouse that always caught her eye. Mostly, because it was home to a herd of adorable harbor seals that loved to hang out on the rocks basking in the sun during certain times of the year.

A sharp bark from Baxter and tug on the leash interrupted Tassie's thoughts and she looked down to see that he'd stopped directly in front of Conrad Meyers' house, his full attention fixed on it. Drats! All she needed was for the man to come out and see them standing there. Never mind that they were on the sidewalk and not even close to his lawn.

Tassie was about to urge Baxter along when she noticed that the front door of the house was slightly open. Like Conrad had either left in a hurry or just gone inside and not realized it hadn't closed behind him. Either way, it was none of her concern.

"Come on, Baxter," she said, leading him forward.

But Baxter didn't budge. Instead, he looked from the house to her and back to the house again.

She followed his gaze with a frown. "What?"

He glanced at her, then gave the house another pointed look.

"The door is open. I know," she said. "So what?"

Baxter let out a little whine.

She shook her head. "No. I'm not telling him that his door is open."

Another whine, this time a little louder.

"Bluewater Bay is a very safe place to live, Baxter. Half the people in town probably don't even lock their doors."

Tassie wasn't sure that part about people not locking their doors was true and from the sideways glance Baxter gave her, he knew it.

She sighed. "Fine! We'll let him know that his door is open. But if Conrad blows a gasket, it's your fault."

Scooping Baxter up in her arms, she made her way up the sidewalk to the house. Baxter's gaze was fixed on the door, ears perked, front paws draped adorably over her forearm as usual whenever she carried him.

She slowed her steps as she got closer to the house in case Conrad came out and started shouting at them. But the house was weirdly quiet.

"Mr. Meyers?" she called.

No answer.

Tassie knocked lightly on the partially open door. "Hello? Mr. Meyers?"

Again, there was no answer.

In her arms, Baxter let out a little yip.

She braced herself, expecting Conrad to storm out from behind whatever rock trolls like him hid behind and rail at them for being on his property, but there wasn't a sound from inside the house.

Okay, this was getting bizarre.

"Clearly, he isn't home, so I'm going to close the door and act like we were never here," she told Baxter softly.

Reaching out, she grasped the knob to do exactly that when she caught sight of a worn boot lying at an angle just inside the doorway—a boot that had a foot in it!

She cautiously pushed the door open a little more.

Conrad Meyers lay on the floor of the entryway, lifeless eyes open and staring at her, a heavy model wooden ship on the floor beside him.

Tassie froze, staring at the blood on the floor and barely visible shoe print, not sure what she was seeing even as her mind began to piece everything together. It wasn't until Baxter let out another little yip that she managed to shake off the shock.

Still holding onto Baxter, she dug her phone out of her purse with a shaking hand and dialed 9-1-1. Lucy immediately answered.

"9-1-1. What's your emergency?"

"Lucy, it's me," Tassie said. "Conrad Meyers is dead. I think someone murdered him."

Chapter 2

Lucy had asked Tassie to wait until the police arrived, so she walked around the front lawn with Baxter, wanting to be as far away from Conrad's body as possible. Even now, she couldn't stand to be near the man. He might be dead, but the way he'd acted toward everyone when he was alive still annoyed her. As for Baxter, he sniffed the grass like he was looking for clues as to who'd killed the creep the whole time.

Yet, while she might not like Conrad, there was something upsetting about his murder anyway. Bluewater Bay was—and always had been—a safe town. People didn't commit murder here. They walked their dogs and took their kids to the playground. They went apple picking and pumpkin picking and enjoyed hayrides at the fall festival. They watched the lobster boat races and took part in the fishing rodeo. They strolled along the boardwalk in the summer and supported the local community theater. But someone most definitely had killed

Conrad. Would any of them be safe until the murderer was caught?

Even though it was broad daylight, she spent most of the time nervously glancing at the house, worried that whoever had done it might still be inside. But that was silly, of course. Baxter would let her know if someone was in there. Regardless, she was relieved when Detective Sterling finally showed up fifteen minutes later. Tall and imposing, he stepped out of his SUV with that air of authority all law enforcement seemed to possess, his calm demeanor contrasting sharply with her own frantic state.

She stared.

Wow.

Lucy was right. Bluewater Bay's new detective, Jack Sterling, *was* cute. Of course, now probably wasn't the time to appreciate his dark hair, dreamy brown eyes, square jaw with that perfect amount of stubble, and broad shoulders. Or that he looked amazing in the navy blue peacoat he was wearing.

No, it most certainly wasn't the time. Not while standing a few feet from Conrad Meyers' dead body anyway.

Dead bodies were a definite mood killer.

In addition to the detective, there was a uniformed officer named Henry Thompson, whom she knew because he'd gone to school with Abby, as well as Dr. Anthony and his dour-faced assistant, Jameson Hall. Emmit Anthony was the town's one and only coroner while his twin brother, Silas, was the town's one and only mortician. Which was kind of disconcerting when she thought about it. A dark, devious place in her mind always wondered if the two of them had a twisted business relationship going on. If Silas needed more work, Dr. Anthony could always kill people and say it was an accidental death.

Okay, so maybe she had an overactive imagination. But weirder things had happened.

All three of them went into the house, leaving her and Baxter outside with Detective Sterling.

"Tassie Drake?" he asked, eyeing her even as he bent to greet Baxter, who happily wagged his tail and tilted his ears back in greeting.

She nodded. "That's me."

"I'm Detective Sterling." He straightened and held out his hand. "You discovered the body?"

Tassie shook his hand, absently noting how warm it was despite the chill in the air. Or maybe it felt warm *because* it was so chilly out. That had to be it. Because it could have nothing to do with the fact that he was hotter than any summer in Maine.

What? Just because she turned down Lucy's offer to introduce her to the newest member of Bluewater Bay's finest didn't mean she couldn't appreciate how handsome he was.

"Yes. In there," she said, gesturing toward Conrad's house.

"Mind walking me through what happened?"

Tassie took a deep breath. "Baxter and I were strolling by when I noticed the door was open, so I thought I should let Conrad know. I called out his name and when I didn't hear anything, I started to close the door, figuring he wasn't home and left it open by mistake."

"Is that when you found Conrad?"

"Yes," she said. "Right inside the entryway."

He jotted down something in the notebook he'd taken out of his pocket, then regarded her curiously. "Did you go into the house?"

"No," she said. "I didn't want to mess up the crime scene."

When he lifted a brow at that, she abruptly realized how weird it had probably sounded. Like she was a cop or something. She reached up with her free hand to tuck her hair behind her ear only to remember she was wearing a hat.

Finding a dead body had her all befuddled.

Or maybe it was simply being this near to Detective Sterling.

She quickly smoothed her hat with her hand, pretending as if she meant to check and make sure it was properly in place the whole time.

"I read a lot of mysteries and watch a lot of them on TV," she explained, feeling her face color. "*Murder She Wrote, Aurora Teagarden, Murder She Baked, Mystery 101.* Pretty much anything and everything on the Hallmark Mysteries Channel. The cops never want anyone touching anything when there's been a murder."

He pondered that for a moment. "How do you know he was murdered?"

"Well, there was blood on the floor and a big heavy-looking model ship beside him. I'm assuming Conrad didn't hit himself on the head."

She thought Detective Sterling might make some crack about the dangers of assuming, but instead he continued to regard her curiously, eyes narrowing a little. "You seem pretty calm for someone who just found a dead body."

Tassie snorted. "That's probably because I didn't exactly like the guy."

His brow arched again, higher this time.

"I mean, nobody in town liked him. Not just me," she added quickly. "But finding a dead body isn't an everyday thing, you know, so I'd be lying if I said I wasn't still a little shaken up. And I wouldn't lie to the police."

That was true.

The detective's mouth twitched. "Fair enough, I suppose. And what time was this?"

She thought a moment, trying to remember when she'd called 9-1-1. She considered taking out her phone to check but then realized she didn't need to because she'd looked at the doggy-themed clock on the wall in Pupcakes before she and Baxter left. It usually took about ten minutes to get to Conrad's house from there. Fifteen if they stopped to talk to people on the way.

"Around two-thirty, I think. Baxter and I left our shop a little after two-fifteen to go to the dog park."

He scribbled some more notes before looking at her again. "What kind of store do you own?"

"Pupcakes," she said with a smile. Talking about her little shop always made her happy. Probably because it paired her two favorite things—dogs and baking. "It's a doggy bakery right in the middle of town."

"Ah. I'll have to stop by with my dog sometime." He flashed her a grin, his eyes holding hers for a moment before he reminded her why they were there. "But back to Conrad. You said that no one in town liked him?"

She made a face. "No one who has a dog at least. Conrad was the quintessential get-off-my-lawn guy. If your dog even stopped to sniff the grass, the creep went ballistic."

Detective Sterling seemed to consider that. "Did you ever have a run-in with him about it?"

"Me? No," she said, reaching down to gently run her hand along Baxter's head and ears. "But I know plenty of people who did."

"Interesting," he said. "Do you think any of them could have been angry enough to murder him?"

Tassie did a double take. "No way. I know almost everyone in town who has a dog and none of them would do something like this, regardless of how much they loathed Conrad."

His mouth curved wryly. "You'd be surprised what someone can do when they're provoked, Ms. Drake."

She considered that. As a detective, he obviously had more experience in that area than she did, but she'd be stunned if someone she knew committed this murder.

"Did you see anyone else as you were walking by the house?" he asked.

"No one."

Detective Sterling took out a business card and offered it to her. "If you think of anything else, give me a call. Or if you—you know—need anything."

Was he flirting with her? And at a crime scene, no less.

Regardless of where they were, she hoped so. He'd already checked the most important box when it came to a guy—he loved dogs. That much was obvious. Not only did he have a pooch, but he'd also greeted Baxter when he'd first arrived.

The card had the Bluewater Bay logo in the top left along with his name and detective rank, as well as the station phone and his cell number in the center.

She smiled, flirting right back. "I will."

Mouth curving, he reached down to pet Baxter before giving her a nod and starting toward the house.

"Actually," Tassie said.

Detective Sterling stopped, turning to look at her.

"Sara Larson, one of my doggy bakery customers spoke to Conrad about an hour before he was murdered. She might have seen someone."

His gaze sharpened at that. "Really?"

Something in his tone made Tassie think he was already considering Sara a suspect. Tassie could practically see the gears turning in his head.

"I'm not saying she did it," Tassie said quickly. "Just—you know—in case she saw something helpful."

He scribbled a note in his pad. "Thanks for the heads up. I'll look into it. If I need more info, I'll be in touch."

Tassie nodded, still a little nervous. Maybe she shouldn't have mentioned Sara.

"Sure thing, Detective. I hope you figure out who did this."

Would it be wrong to add she'd like to thank that person for making the walk to the dog park a lot easier for everyone now that they wouldn't have to worry about accidentally stepping foot on that insufferable creep's lawn and getting called every nasty name in the book?

Probably.

He flashed her a smile. "Stay out of trouble, Ms. Drake."

Tassie wanted to tell him that he didn't have to worry about that because she never got *into* trouble, but Detective Sterling had already disappeared inside the house. She bet he hadn't expected to have a murder to solve his first day on the job in Bluewater Bay. And considering how fast news traveled in their sleepy little town, word of Conrad's murder would be everywhere by the time she and Baxter got back to Pupcakes.

That could either make the detective's job harder or easier, she supposed.

Chapter 3

"You know, when I offered to introduce you to Jack, I didn't mean meeting him at a crime scene," Lucy said dryly.

Tassie made a face as she speared a cherry tomato with her fork. "Very funny."

Lucy had gotten chicken Parmesan with whole grain pasta and a side salad delivered from the best Italian restaurant in Bluewater Bay, and the aroma of garlic and marinara sauce filled the kitchen. With it's white cabinets, light blue subway tile backsplash, and pot rack hanging above the small island in the center, the room seemed bigger than it actually was thanks to the open floor plan of the house. While Lucy was a lot of amazing things, a chef wasn't one of them. Which was why her husband pretty much did all the cooking in their house. Tassie could say first-hand that it was true what they said about firefighters being excellent cooks. He made some killer meals.

"I was right, though, wasn't I?" Lucy asked, not fazed in the slightest by Tassie's snark.

"About what?" Tassie asked.

Her friend picked up her glass of water and gestured with it. "About Jack being cute."

To Tassie's right, Abby shook her head with a snort. "You do know you're a married woman, right?"

"Of course, I know, which is why I was vetting Jack for your sister and not me." Lucy gave Tassie a pointed look. "You still haven't answered my question."

Tassie took her time slathering a piece of mozzarella-covered chicken in more marinara before replying. "Yes, you were right. Detective Sterling *is* very cute."

Although, now that she thought about it, maybe *cute* wasn't the right word.

Attractive.

Handsome.

Gorgeous.

Those were much better words.

On the other side of the table, Lucy gave her a smug smile. "Nothing says romance like crime scene tape and chalk outlines."

Tassie could only roll her eyes.

Abby twirled some saucy pasta on her fork. "I don't know how you even noticed what the new guy looked like after finding a dead body. I would have been way too freaked out."

"Even if the dead body in question was Conrad Meyers?" Tassie asked.

Abby thought a moment as she chewed, then finally shrugged. "Good point. But still...a dead body, Tassie."

"Yeah, I know." Tassie agreed, letting out a sigh. "Trust me. It wasn't exactly the highlight of my day."

Even if she did get to meet the newest and decidedly most attractive member of Bluewater Bay's finest.

Lucy helped herself to some more salad. "Who do you think did it? I mean, half of Bluewater Bay probably wanted to off Conrad at one time or another, especially anyone who had to walk by his house to get to the dog park."

Tassie poured more iced tea into her glass from the pitcher on the table. "That's what I told Detective Sterling. Although, I regretted mentioning it right away. I honestly hope the murderer isn't one of the bakery's customers."

"Well, whoever it is, they should get a medal," Lucy said, gesturing with her fork. "If you ask me, they did this town a favor."

Abby giggled. "I can see the headline now. *Local Hero Commits Murder; Town Gives Them a Medal.*"

Tassie burst out laughing, unable to help herself. It was probably wrong to speak ill of a man who'd just been murdered, but considering how hateful to everyone he'd been, could anyone really blame her?

"In all seriousness though, I don't know one person in town who liked Conrad," Lucy continued. "And that was before he won all those millions in the lottery."

"I heard he didn't even share any of the money with his son," Abby said, finishing the last of her salad. "Can you believe that?"

Tassie snorted. "I can believe it. I'm pretty sure that creep didn't have a generous bone in his body. Why the heck his ex-wife ever married him is beyond me."

"Maybe he wasn't always a jerk," her sister suggested.

"Then again," Lucy pointed out, "the woman is his *ex*-wife, so maybe he was."

Tassie sipped her iced tea. "Enough about Conrad. Let's talk about something more fun." She gave Lucy a pointed look. "Like whether you and Andrew have decided on a name for the baby yet."

Her friend made a face. "Ugh. Not yet. We can't agree on any of them. But on the bright side, we've come up with a way to finally settle on one."

"Please don't say you're going to flip a quarter," Tassie said dryly.

Lucy laughed. "No. Something even better. We're going to have everyone at the baby shower write a name on a piece of paper and put it in a hat, then pick one out, and whatever it is, that's what we'll call the baby."

Tassie exchanged looks with Abby to see that her sister was as stunned as she was. Even Baxter and Finn, who were sitting on the floor beside the table, seemed dubious. From the expression on Lucy's dog's face, Bruno the Basset Hound had already heard the idea and clearly thought it was as fraught with danger as the rest of them.

"You can't be serious," Tassie said.

"Of course, I am." Lucy frowned. "Why wouldn't I be?"

"Because someone could pick a name that you and Andrew hate," Tassie said, pointing out the obvious.

"Or pick a weird name that's a string of Greek letters with a hyphen somewhere in between," Abby added.

Lucy waved her hand dismissively. "Everyone coming to the baby shower is either family or a friend. They aren't going to do that to us."

Beside her chair, Baxter gazed up at Tassie doubtfully. She shared the sentiment. But Lucy always did do things a little differently.

"Speaking of the baby shower," Lucy said, looking at Tassie. "Are you sure you don't need help putting it together? I'd be glad to give you a hand."

Tassie had started planning the baby shower from the moment Lucy told her that she was pregnant. While she still had a lot to do, Tassie already had Sara making the party favors—cute homemade teddy bear soaps that smelled like baby powder—and Gwen was making assorted flavors of cupcakes decorated with equally adorable teddy bears. Unfortunately, Tassie hadn't quite nailed down the menu or chosen a restaurant to cater the party. Or gotten the decorations yet. But in her defense, she'd been super busy at the bakery with multiple birthday party orders as well as getting everything ready for Bluewater Bay's popular Dog Days event, which was happening a few weeks after Lucy's baby shower.

So, yeah, it was a little hectic right now.

"I know," Tassie said. "But what kind of godmother would I be to your sweet little boy if I let his mother help with her own baby shower?"

"A busy one," Lucy insisted.

Tassie smiled. "Who is never too busy for my best friend, but if I need help, I promise to ask."

That seemed to satisfy her friend. "Okay. But you'd better!"

Tassie glanced at Abby. "How'd things go with Isaac?"

Her sister had hurried out to make her appointment with the dog psychologist the moment Tassie had gotten back to the store that afternoon and then they'd both met up at Lucy's, so she hadn't gotten a chance to find out what had happened.

"Who's Isaac?" Lucy asked, looking back and forth between them curiously.

"A good-looking dog psychologist who Abby's attracted to," Tassie said simply. "But instead of asking him out for coffee, she's decided to take Finn for therapy so she and Isaac can get to know each other first."

Lucy considered that, a confused look on her face. "Won't a dog psychologist figure out pretty quickly that Finn doesn't have any behavioral issues?"

Tassie nodded. "That's what I said."

"He did." Abby let out a sigh. "And now Isaac thinks I'm the one who needs therapy because I'm not projecting the right kind of energy with Finn. Which was true, I guess. At least when I was there. I mean, I was acting all weird. Even poor Finn noticed." She reached down to run her free hand over her Dachshund's head. "Sorry, boy. But on the bright side, we have another session with Isaac."

Lucy shook her head. "Well, this isn't the craziest thing you've ever done to meet a guy." She looked at Tassie. "Remember in middle school when Abby talked your mom and dad into getting her an oboe because the boy she liked was in the band and she ended up passing out trying to play the darn thing?"

"I remember." Tassie couldn't help grinning at Abby. Or teasing her big sis. "How about in high school when you went to get a tattoo because the guy you were crushing on was into them?"

Abby groaned. "At least I was eighteen and didn't try to use a fake ID or anything. But yeah, I remember. Unfortunately, now I have one little ink dot on my ankle instead of the flower I wanted because getting a tattoo hurt too much. This isn't the same thing though."

"If you say so," Lucy muttered. "But if you ask me, I think this is all going to blow up in your face."

"Lucy's right," Tassie said. "Just be honest with him, Abbs. Tell Isaac that the whole thing was a pretense so you could meet him. Then ask him to grab coffee."

Her sister's brows drew together as she considered that, but before she could say anything one way or another, Tassie's ringing cell phone interrupted the conversation. She glanced over at where it lay on the table near her plate to see Sara's name on the screen.

She looked at Lucy and held up her finger. "Hold that thought."

Picking up her phone, Tassie thumbed the green button and held it to her ear. "Hey, Sara. What's up?"

She hoped there wasn't an issue with the teddy bear soaps for the baby shower. She really had her heart set on them.

"Tassie! Thank goodness you answered." Sara sounded as flustered as she had that afternoon at the bakery. In fact, it sounded like she was bordering on tears. "The police are arresting me for Conrad Meyers' murder."

Tassie did a double take. Surely, she hadn't heard that right. "What?!"

"I know. I can't believe it either," Sara said, voice trembling. "Can you come over and get Roxie? I was hoping you could babysit her for me."

Beside Tassie's chair, Baxter immediately got to his feet, ears alert.

"Yes, of course," she said. "I'll be right there."

Still stunned, Tassie hung up. The amusing discussion about picking baby names, whether she needed help with the shower, and her sister's guy problems suddenly felt like a distant memory. This couldn't be happening, right?

"What is it?" Lucy asked, the same concern on her face mirrored in Abby's eyes as well.

Tassie quickly filled them in as she pushed back her chair and headed into the living room where she'd left her purse on one of the two swivel cushion chairs near the stone fireplace, Baxter prancing along at her side.

"Do you want us to come with you?" Abby asked, she and Lucy following at her heels.

She shook her head and gave them a small smile. "Thanks, but I'm good. I'll call you guys once I find out what's going on with Sara. Hopefully, this is all some big misunderstanding."

Chapter 4

"The police can't really think that Sara murdered Conrad, can they?"

From where he sat in the safety of his doggy car carrier in her SUV, Baxter gave Tassie what could only be described as a worried look.

"I know. I'm concerned too," she muttered, then quickly added, "Not because I think Sara did it, but because the police think she did."

Tassie clicked on her indicator, then slowed at the next street and turned right. Sara's place was only about fifteen minutes from Lucy's house so luckily, it didn't take long to get there.

"Why *do* the police think Sara did it anyway?" she mused to Baxter. "Sara didn't even know him. Heck, she didn't even run into Conrad other than whenever she walked by his house with Roxie on the way to the dog park."

The whole thing simply didn't add up.

Sara lived in a one-bedroom studio apartment on the north side of town. The building—like many in Bluewater Bay—had been recognized by the historical society, meaning that while the exterior had been refurbished, the building had to maintain the original style, architecture, and colors. Tassie had to admit the gabled roof and clapboard painted Wedgwood blue were pretty stunning.

Sara's car was in her reserved parking space, but there weren't any police cars around—unless you counted Detective Sterling's SUV.

Pulling into one of the guest parking spaces, Tassie attached Baxter's leash to his harness, then looped her crossbody bag over her shoulder and headed toward the building.

Sara's apartment was on the third floor halfway down the hallway. When she and Baxter reached it, Tassie knocked on the door, then anxiously waited. If Detective Sterling were the only one here, maybe she could talk him out of arresting Sara for Conrad's murder before he took her to jail.

Tassie was just about to knock again when the door opened. Jack Sterling stood there looking as handsome as he had earlier when she'd seen him at Conrad's house. In the soft glow from the floor lamp just inside the doorway, his brown eyes reminded her of the delicious imported Belgian chocolate she sometimes splurged on.

"Ms. Drake," he said. "Come in."

"Detective."

She walked past him, Baxter right beside her.

Usually so warm and welcoming, Sara's cute apartment seemed somehow a little less cheerful even though the familiar comforting scent of essential oils she used in her soaps lingered in the air. Vanilla, lavender, and patchouli combined into a delightful mix, filling the space.

Roxie immediately jumped off the couch and ran over to greet them, touching her nose to Baxter's. Tassie crouched to run her hand over Roxie's wiry fur. "It's okay. Baxter and I are here now."

Straightening, she looked around. The kitchen, living room, and bedroom were combined into one big colorful area, but Sara was nowhere to be seen.

She turned back around to face Detective Sterling. "Where's Sara?"

"An officer already took her down to the station for booking."

Drats. So much for talking him out of arresting Sara.

Tassie folded her arms and pinned him with a look. "Mind explaining why my friend is behind bars for Conrad's murder?"

In the back of her mind, she remembered her grandmother telling her when she was a little girl that she'd get more with honey than she would with vinegar, but right now, she wasn't eager to pick up their flirting where she and Detective Sterling had left off that afternoon. Her friend might be facing life in prison for a murder she didn't commit.

Baxter gazed up at the detective, clearly as interested in the answer to that question as she was.

"Because we have evidence," he said simply.

"Evidence?" Tassie scoffed. "Against Sara? She might not have liked Conrad, but murder? I don't buy that."

Jack took a deep breath and gestured toward the couch. "Let's sit down and talk."

"The evidence you have is so bad that I need to sit down?" she practically squeaked. "What, are you afraid I'm going to pass out or something?"

He didn't say anything, but simply gestured to the couch again.

Worried they might be a while, Tassie unhooked Baxter's leash from his harness and sat down on one end of the couch, while Detective Sterling took the other. Baxter and Roxie immediately jumped up to sit on the cushions between them. The detective reached out to pet Roxie even as Tassie did the same to Baxter. She might be annoyed with the man right now—he *did* just wrongly arrest her friend regardless of whatever evidence he had—but it was obvious to her once again he had a soft spot for animals.

So, there was that.

"I spoke to Conrad's next-door neighbor after talking to you at the crime scene and she said that she saw Sara arguing with him right before he was murdered," Detective Sterling said.

Tassie made a face. "Everyone who walked by Conrad's house with their dog argued with him at one time or another. If you go by that, you'd have to arrest more than half the town."

"Maybe," he agreed. "But not everyone followed him into his house to continue fighting with him."

"Wait. What?" Tassie stared at him in disbelief. "Sara was *in* his house?"

Why hadn't her friend mentioned that? Unless…

No. Sara did *not* kill Conrad. She wouldn't believe that.

Detective Sterling nodded. "Yes. Then, a little while later, she came running out."

Tassie took a deep breath. Then another.

"Okay," she said slowly. "But that doesn't necessarily indicate she killed Conrad. I mean, someone could have gone into the house and killed him after Sara left. Right?"

"It's possible," he agreed. "But the coroner puts the time of death right around the time that the neighbor saw Sara leave and she didn't see anyone else go inside after that. Tassie, this isn't the first time the woman saw them fighting. And it's not the first time Sara followed him into his house. The same neighbor saw her there at least one other time. We have a pattern here."

Tassie's mind raced as she grappled with that revelation. Why would Sara be visiting Conrad, especially when arguing with him upset her so much? None of this made sense.

"A pattern still doesn't mean she killed him, Detective. Sara might have hated Conrad, but to say that she murdered him is a stretch to say the least. I don't care how many times that neighbor saw her go into his house."

He sighed. "Sara's fingerprints were on the murder weapon."

Tassie opened her mouth, then closed it again, not sure what to say. That information was a little harder to discredit. Beside her, Baxter leaned in close, resting his front paws on her lap and nuzzling her with his nose. She ran her hand over his silky head.

"I don't know why her fingerprints would be on the murder weapon, but I'm sure there's a good explanation," she finally managed, wishing she could offer him that better *explanation* right now. "What about that shoe print? Did you check to make sure it matched Sara's shoes? Because she didn't have blood on them when she came into Pupcakes."

He looked at her in surprise. "How did you know about the shoe print?"

"I noticed it when Baxter and I found Conrad's body," she said. "I told you that I watch a lot of mysteries. So did it match Sara's shoes?"

"No," he said. "But since it was only a partial print, it wasn't much help in that area."

Tassie didn't say anything.

Detective Sterling leaned forward, his gaze unwavering. "I get it. Friends want to defend each other. But I have a job to do, and that job includes putting murderers in prison."

"Well, Henry wouldn't have arrested Sara."

In all honesty, she wasn't sure what the town's former detective would have done in this situation. He'd never had to investigate a murder.

Scooping Baxter up in her arms, Tassie shot to her feet and glared down at Detective Sterling. "I don't care what you think. I know Sara, and she's not a killer."

And she was going to prove it.

Tassie clipped Baxter's leash on his harness, then picked up Roxie's from the hook beside the door where Sara always kept it and hooked it onto the harness the Jack Russel was already wearing. When she was finished, she turned to Detective Sterling.

"What happens to Sara now?" she asked.

"She'll be arraigned in the morning and most likely make bail," he said, getting to his feet. "After that, it's up to her lawyer."

She frowned. "That's it? You aren't even going to entertain the possibility that Sara didn't do it and keep looking for the person who actually did?"

The detective gave her a thoughtful look. "If new evidence comes to light, then yes."

But would he look for that new evidence?

One leash in either hand, Tassie lifted her chin. "Well, then I guess now I have a job to do too."

He lifted a brow, a move that made her pulse skip a beat because he looked even more handsome when he did it despite how annoyed and frustrated she was with him at the moment.

"What job is that?" he asked.

"Finding out who really killed Conrad and clearing Sara's name."

With that, Tassie stormed out of the apartment, Baxter on one side of her and Roxie on the other, leaving Detective Sterling to think whatever he liked. She might not be a cop like him, but she was determined to figure out who murdered Conrad.

And she'd always been very good at solving mysteries.

Well, at least the ones on TV.

Chapter 5

Roxie was the perfect little house guest. And since Tassie shared a condo with Abby, both Baxter and Finn got to play with Sara's dog. But ever since they'd all arrived at Pupcakes the next morning, poor Roxie kept looking out the windows at everyone who walked by, searching for her mommy. It was all so confusing for the little girl.

Honestly, Tassie was wondering where Sara was too. According to Lucy, Sara had made bail a little before noon. That was almost an hour ago. Maybe there was a lot of paperwork to fill out. Or she could be strategizing with her lawyer. Tassie had never been arrested, so she wasn't sure.

Telling herself that had to be it, Tassie finished rolling out the dough she'd just made, the aroma of peanut butter and cinnamon wafting up to her nose. Picking up the squirrel-shaped cookie cutter, she pressed it carefully into the dough, then transferred the doggy treats to the metal tray. The repetitive motion helped keep her mind off Sara and her predicament.

As Tassie had expected, the whole town was talking about the murder. Not surprisingly, everyone seemed genuinely stunned that the police thought Sara killed Conrad. On the flip side, they also said they could understand if she had. It was the main topic of conversation among Pupcakes' customers today, that was for sure.

And maybe their dogs, too, if the looks poor Roxie was sending their way was any indication. More likely though, she was simply anxious about Sara.

As if on cue, the door to the shop opened and Sara walked in. Her eyes were red, like she'd been crying and her face was pale. All in all, she looked exhausted and completely wrung out. And who could blame her? She'd been arrested for murder and spent the night in a jail cell.

Tassie put the tray of doggy cookies she'd just made into the oven and turned on the timer, then quickly stripped off the disposable vinyl gloves she wore when she baked, tossing them in the trash can as she moved out from behind the counter to greet Sara. Roxie beat her to it, tail wagging happily at the sight of her mommy. Sara immediately picked her up, hugging her close and burying her face against Roxie's fur.

The sight made Tassie's heart squeeze. Sara couldn't go to prison. Poor Roxie would be devastated.

Sara gave Tassie a small smile as she walked over. "Thank you for babysitting Roxie."

"Of course." Tassie returned her smile, leaning in to give her a hug. "Are you okay?"

Dumb question. Sara was being accused of murder. Who'd be okay with that?

"I'm better now," Sara said softly, caressing Roxie's fur even as she nervously took in all of the people in the store.

People who were eyeing Sara with a mix of compassion and pity. While Tassie was sure Sara would appreciate their kind words and offers of support, she wasn't sure her friend could handle it right now.

"Let's go in the back," Tassie said, putting her hand on Sara's arm and urging her in that direction.

Catching Abby's eye, Tassie motioned toward the break room as they went, Baxter falling into step beside her, butt wiggling and tail high in the air.

The break room at Pupcakes was part kitchenette and part doggy playroom. The big plush chairs, comfy dog donut beds, and colorful decor were eclectic to say the least, but somehow, they worked.

Tassie slalomed her way through the stuffed doggy toys on the floor, glancing over her shoulder. "Want some tea?"

Sara sank down onto one of the lavender colored stuffed chairs with a grateful sigh. "I'd love some. Thanks."

Tassie opened the fancy bamboo tea box Lucy had gotten her and Abby when they'd opened the store and took out two bags of green tea, then filled the electric kettle and turned it on. Her grandmother used to say that tea always tasted better when you heated the water in a kettle instead of the microwave. Tassie wasn't quite sure about that, but the tea kettle reminded her of her nana whenever she used it—even if it wasn't the old-fashioned kind that went on top of the stove—so she opted for it over the microwave all the time. Even now, despite everything going on with Sara, Tassie couldn't help smiling a little.

When the water was hot, she poured it into the mugs with the tea bags, then carried them over to the low table along with some sweetener packets. Sitting down in the other chair, Tassie opened two of the packs and sprinkled it in her tea.

Sara sweetened her own tea before picking up the mug and taking a slow sip. Cup in hand, she sat back in the chair. "This is just what I needed. Thank you."

"I still can't believe the police arrested you," Tassie said, getting comfortable in her own chair.

On his round, fluffy bed on the floor, Baxter seemed to be listening with half an ear while he chewed on a stuffed squirrel. As for Roxie, she'd taken up residence beside Sara's chair, head resting on her paws as she relaxed.

Sara gazed down at her mug thoughtfully. "When they came to my apartment, I thought Detective Sterling wanted to ask me some more questions. I never thought he was there to arrest me for murder." She looked at Tassie. "I didn't kill Conrad."

Tassie glanced at Baxter to see if her friend was lying, then immediately felt badly about it. She was relieved when her pup continued to chew on his toy instead of giving her his patented side-eye look. Of course, Sara didn't kill anyone!

She reached over to give Sara's hand a comforting squeeze. "I already knew that. And so does everyone who knows you."

Sara nodded and gave her a small smile. "That didn't stop my lawyer from trying to talk me into taking a plea deal for a reduced sentence. He wants me to admit to something I didn't do so we can avoid a trial."

Drats. If he was suggesting that, then he must feel like the police had an open-and-shut case against Sara. This was looking worse by the minute.

"You aren't thinking of doing that, right?" Tassie asked.

"No. My boyfriend said his buddy, Warren, is a very good lawyer, and I'm sure he is, but I won't confess to something I didn't do."

While Tassie was relieved to hear that, all she could focus on was a certain tidbit of other information that Sara had let slip. "Wait a minute. You have a boyfriend? When did you start seeing someone? And why didn't I know about this?"

Sara blushed a little and reached up to tuck her hair behind her ear. "Tristan and I just started dating a little while ago."

That wasn't a very common name and there was only one Tristan that Tassie knew about in Bluewater Bay. He was a guitar player and lead singer of the band, The

Grunge Collective, that played at a club called Breakers in town.

He was also...

"Conrad Meyer's son?" she practically squeaked.

Sara's face colored even more as she held up a hand. "I know what you're thinking. But Tristan isn't like his father. He's sweet and kind and he loves animals."

"I wasn't thinking that at all. I know you wouldn't date him if he was anything like Conrad. I was thinking that it must be awkward dating the son of the man whom people think you murdered."

"Tristan knows I didn't kill him," Sara said.

Considering his friend was Sara's lawyer, Tassie figured as much. But still, the whole coincidence was kind of crazy.

"Detective Sterling said that Conrad's neighbor saw you follow him into his house yesterday," Tassie said quietly. "Is that true?"

Sara hesitated for a moment, but then nodded.

Drats. Tassie had been hoping the neighbor got that wrong.

"Why did you do that?" she asked.

Sara reached down to pet Roxie, her expression distant. "He said all these hateful things about Roxie then just turned and walked away like it was nothing. I don't know what I was trying to accomplish by continuing to fight with him. It was dumb."

"Okay. You were defending Roxie. I get that," Tassie said. "But what about the other time you followed him into his house?"

Her friend looked at her sharply. "You know about that?"

Tassie nodded. "Detective Sterling told me. That same neighbor saw you."

Sara let out a groan, sinking deeper into her chair, shoulders slumping. "A few weeks ago, Tristan and I stopped by Conrad's house on the way to the dog park. Knowing how much Conrad hated dogs anywhere near his lawn, I told Tristan that maybe I should wait out on the sidewalk while he went to see what his father wanted to talk to him about, but he said it'd be fine. That his father wouldn't say anything if Roxie and I were with him."

"But Conrad did?"

"Yeah," Sara said. "Conrad flew off the handle the minute Tristan and I walked around to the backyard even though I was holding Roxie. When he said he didn't want Roxie and me there, Tristan got into this big fight with him. Conrad said some pretty ugly things to Tristan before we left."

Since most everyone got on the receiving end of Conrad's bad temper, why not his son? Still, that was still harsh.

"Anyway," Sara continued. "After we went to the dog park, Tristan had to get to rehearsal with the guys in the band, so I dropped Roxie off at my place, then went back to talk to Conrad. I wanted to make him see how much he'd hurt Tristan, but he didn't want to hear it. That's when I picked up that stupid model ship and left my fingerprints all over it. I was emphasizing my point to Conrad that he put more importance on stuff like that than he did his own son. I finally realized I was wasting my breath, so I left."

Tassie *knew* there was a good explanation for Sara's prints being on the murder weapon. "Did you tell Detective Sterling any of this?"

Sara nodded. "And my lawyer, too. Warren said that it only makes me look like more of a suspect because I had a problem with Conrad."

From their point of view, Tassie supposed she could understand that. But just because Sara had an issue with Conrad doesn't automatically make her a murderer.

"The police will find the real murderer, Sara," Tassie said. "You'll see."

Her friend nodded, but she didn't look convinced.

Sighing, Tassie offered her a small smile she hoped was reassuring. "Tell me about Tristan. How did the two of you meet?"

Sara's lips curved, her face immediately brightening. "At Hug in a Mug. We bumped into each other—literally. We both go there to get coffee practically every day but that was the first time we ever saw each other. We got to talking, then met up later for dinner before going to Breakers so I could listen to his band."

"Sounds like all the makings of a great first date to me," Tassie said with a grin.

Sara laughed. "It was." Then she sighed, her face clouding with worry. "I really like him, Tassie—a lot. And now I might go to jail for the rest of my life for murdering his father." She looked down at her dog, eyes filling with tears. "What about poor Roxie? I'm the only mommy she's ever known. If I go to prison…" She shook her head. "I know you said the police will find the real murderer, but what if they don't?"

"They will," Tassie said firmly. "And if they don't, then I'll do it."

Her friend stared at her in obvious confusion. "You?"

"Yes, me. I'm going to find out who the real killer is. Because I'm not letting my friend go to prison."

Chapter 6

"Are you sure this is a good idea?" Abby asked.

Tassie was taking advantage of the afternoon lull in customers to fill in her sister—as well as Lucy, who'd stopped by on her break—on her plan to uncover the real murderer.

"Am I sure? No," Tassie said. "Am I doing it anyway? Yes."

Lucy frowned at her over the rim of the cup of ginger tea she'd gotten from Hug in a Mug, which was directly across the street from Pupcakes. "This isn't an episode of *Murder She Wrote*. Going after a killer is dangerous. You know that, right?"

Murder She Wrote was one of Tassie's comfort shows. The mysteries were fun, and Jessica Fletcher always figured out who the killer was. She made it all look very easy, too. Tassie wasn't dumb. She knew it wouldn't be that simple in real life, but she had to try anyway.

Over by where he was sniffing around the display case that showcased the various doggy birthday-slash-gotcha-day cakes and cookies Pupcakes sold, Baxter perked up his ears in their direction with an expression that suggested he was siding with Abby and Lucy on this. That was probably because he'd seen every episode of *Murder She Wrote* right along with Tassie.

"I know, but I have to do this. I have to," Tassie said, as much to make Baxter understand as Abby and Lucy. She sighed. "Sara got arrested because of me."

They both frowned this time, clearly confused.

"What are you talking about?" Abby asked.

Tassie hesitated, ashamed to admit how stupid she'd been. "I told Detective Sterling that Sara spoke to Conrad right before he was murdered because I thought she might have *seen* something to help him with his investigation. I never dreamed Conrad's neighbor heard Sara fighting with him and then running out of his house around the time he was murdered."

There. She'd said it. The whole ugly truth.

"You didn't get Sara arrested. You simply told Jack what Sara told you," Lucy said. "He arrested Sara because a witness heard her fighting with Conrad, then running out of his house."

Baxter pranced over to jump into Tassie's lap where she sat on the highboy chair behind the counter where the cash register was. The unconditional love in his beautiful brown eyes made her heart squeeze in her chest. She booped his nose with hers, then pressed a kiss to the top of his head.

"While you could be right—and I'm not saying you are—I still have to help Sara any way I can. She didn't kill Conrad," Tassie finally said. "But I promise I'll be careful. All I'm going to do is ask around town and see if anyone knows anything."

Abby and Lucy exchanged looks.

"What can we do to help?" Abby asked after a moment.

Tassie thought a moment. Investigating Conrad's murder was going to take up a huge chunk of time, there was no doubt about it. She hated the idea of abandoning her sister and the store though.

"What about your session with Isaac?" Tassie asked.

Her sister waved a hand. "Finn and I are seeing him tomorrow, so I'm free."

"Okay," Tassie said. "We've got orders for a few doggy birthday parties I was going to work on, so could you take care of those?"

Abby nodded. "I can do that. What about the baby shower?"

Tassie stifled a groan. Planning Lucy's upcoming baby shower, on the other hand, was going to be a lot trickier. She couldn't put that on Abby's plate too. "I was supposed to check out some restaurants about catering, so I guess I'll do that in between investigating."

Maybe she could invite everyone on her suspect list out to lunch at the various restaurants she was thinking about having cater the party. Who in this town didn't love a good lobster roll? Well, except her, of course.

"Or I could do it for you," Lucy offered excitedly.

"You're determined to plan your own baby shower, aren't you?" Tassie asked.

Her eyes twinkled. "I'm determined to help *you* plan it."

Tassie shook her head, half-exasperated, half-amused. "Okay. I'll text you the names of the restaurants."

"Excellent!" Lucy grinned, clearly reveling in her win. "So, where are you going to start? Investigating, I mean."

That was a good question. And the answer to it was simple so she didn't have to think about it for long.

"I'm going to talk to the neighbor who told the police she saw Sara fighting with Conrad," Tassie told them. "She said she didn't see anyone else going into or leaving the house, but maybe she did and it slipped her mind or something."

Considering the woman was talking to Detective Handsome at the time, Tassie supposed that was understandable. The man had the ability to be very distracting.

"It's worth a try," Lucy said. "Keep us in the loop."

"I will." She kissed Baxter on top of his nose. "Come on, baby. Let's go for a walk."

Chapter 7

Margot Henderson's home was as warm and inviting on the outside as Conrad's was cold and unfriendly. In addition to the colorful bird feeders in front of the big picture window, several garden statues were nestled in the sweeping flowerbeds among the golden yellow witch hazel shrubs. Tassie spotted a bunny, a cat, and a few gnomes among the collection. The fact that the houses were right beside each other made the contrast even more jarring.

"Okay, Baxter," she said, heading up the walkway toward the house. "Time to do our best Jessica Fletcher impersonation."

Taking a deep breath, she pressed the bell and waited.

The door opened a few moments later to reveal a slim woman of about seventy with glasses. She wore her silver hair in a braid over one shoulder and held a plump tabby cat in her arms that regarded them with a lazy curiosity that only a feline could manage. The woman gave Tassie a smile, and an even bigger one to Baxter.

"Ms. Henderson?" Tassie asked.

"Yes," she said, the friendly smile never leaving her face.

"I'm Tassie Drake. I'm a friend of Sara Larson."

Arms still around her cat, she shook her head with a sigh. "That poor girl. Such dreadful business. I can't believe the police think she murdered Conrad."

Tassie grimaced a little. "You and me both. I was wondering if I could talk to you about Conrad if you have a minute."

"Of course." She gave Tassie an apologetic look. "Conrad and I weren't exactly friendly, but I'll tell you anything I can. Come in."

Smiling in thanks, Tassie led Baxter inside.

Margot Henderson's home was—in a word—charming. Two rose-colored couches with embroidered pillows sat perpendicular to the fireplace and the TV above it, an antique white coffee table in between them. A big knitting basket was beside the arm of the couch opposite the picture window, which meant that was probably where the older woman mostly sat, while a tall cat tree occupied the space behind the other couch so her tabby could gaze out at the birds on the feeders as well as the sidewalk and whoever walked past. Framed photos of what were most certainly family and friends lined the mantel as well as filled the walls to either side.

Closing the door, Margot set her cat down on the floor. "Now you behave yourself, Bella. We have guests." She glanced at Tassie. "I was about to have some coffee. Would you like a cup? It's decaf."

Tassie nodded. She was more of a tea girl herself, but she needed to get information from Margot, so she'd have whatever the woman was having.

Unless it was alcohol. She really wasn't much of a drinker. A few sips and she'd dissolve into fits of giggles and forget why she was here.

"Coffee would be great. Thanks."

Despite the friendly way Baxter was wagging his tail, Bella eyed him from a wary distance, then sidled over to the cat tower and made her way to the highest perch with an agility that all cats appeared to possess so she could gaze out at the birds. Baxter, who was no slouch when it came to jumping on stuff, seemed to be seriously contemplating joining Bella, simply to see if the feline jungle gym was as much fun as it looked.

Laughing, Tassie guided him away from temptation and followed Margot into the kitchen. They had work to do.

The walls in the kitchen were the lightest of blues while the cabinets were a soft sage green and the two highboy chairs at the small island in the center were painted a happy lilac. Tassie would never in a million years think about decorating a kitchen in that combination of colors but she had to admit that it all worked.

"Did you know Conrad well?" Tassie asked as she added sweetener to her coffee followed by as much milk as she could manage to fit in the mug.

Margot slid onto the highboy beside her, setting a plate of cookies on the island that were unmistakably from

Dreamy Desserts. Tassie helped herself to a chocolate chunk.

"Well enough to know that I didn't like him," Margot said, then cringed as she picked up a cookie. "I'm sorry. I probably shouldn't say that about a man who's just been murdered, but Conrad was a terrible person."

Tassie sipped her coffee. Someone else in Bluewater Bay who thought Conrad was a jerk. What a surprise.

"It must have been difficult living next door to him," she said.

Margot let out a delicate snort. "That's putting it mildly. He complained every time I filled the bird feeders out front, insisting that it brought squirrels and chipmunks. He didn't care for them in his yard, you see. He said they were always digging up the grass to hide nuts. I told him that squirrels and chipmunks have as much right to live here as we do. What Conrad didn't seem to understand was that those same critters would run around his yard whether I put food out or not." She took a sip of her coffee. "He got even angrier about it over the past few weeks. Every time a squirrel stepped foot in his backyard, he ran outside to chase the poor thing off. He said it was because he didn't want them digging up the golden glow seeds he just planted. I told him it was way too early to plant anything yet, but did he listen? Of course not."

"I'm afraid I wouldn't know myself," Tassie admitted. "I'm not much of a gardener."

To be honest, she wasn't even sure what golden glow were. Some kind of flowers maybe?

"Neither was Conrad." Margot thought a moment, her eyes taking on a distant look as she frowned. "Come to think of it, that's the first time I've ever seen him plant anything."

Maybe he *wasn't* planting anything. Maybe he was hiding all that money he won in the lottery. She could certainly see him doing something like that.

Margot waved her hand dismissively. "Anyway, living next door to Conrad wasn't quite as bad before his wife and son left. Belinda was a sweetheart—still is—and Tristan was a darling little boy. He used to come over to my house all the time." She sighed. "I don't know how Belinda put up with that man for as long as she did. If it were me, I probably would have ended up killing Conrad years ago."

She said the words so casually that she might have been talking about filling those cute bird feeders of hers. But she was obviously speaking hypothetically.

Right?

There was no way Tassie could imagine a sweet older woman like Margot bludgeoning someone.

"Why are you so interested in Conrad, if I may ask?"

Tassie almost choked on her coffee at the question. She should have anticipated Margot asking that. In fact, she was surprised the woman hadn't asked her that very thing the moment she stepped inside.

Beside her, Margot seemed curious but not overly suspicious.

Tassie leveled her gaze at the woman. "I'm trying to find out who murdered him."

Margot didn't so much as blink at that. Instead, she picked up her mug and calmly sipped her coffee. "Isn't that the job of the police?"

"It is," Tassie said. "But in this case, they might need a little help since they think Sara is the one who killed Conrad."

"Ah." Margot set her cup down, realization dawning on her face. "And they think so because I told that nice, new detective that I saw Sara coming out of Conrad's house a little while before he was murdered. I never meant to imply she was the killer. Only that she might have some idea who the murderer was since she was probably one of the last people to see the man alive."

"Unfortunately, they arrested her instead." Tassie let out a sigh. "Are you sure you didn't see anyone else go into or come out of Conrad's house yesterday?"

Margot shook her head. "I wasn't staring out the window all day, but I definitely didn't see anyone around the time Conrad was killed. I'm sorry I can't be of more help."

Well, drats.

"Me, too." Tassie slid off the chair and gave the woman a smile. "Thank you for the coffee and the cookies."

Picking up Baxter's leash, Tassie started to follow Margot into the living room when she caught sight of two twenty-five-pound bags of birdseed in the mud room off the kitchen. There was nothing remarkable about them really, other than the fact that they were heavy. Especially for a person Margot's age.

"You don't carry those bags of birdseed into the house from your car by yourself, do you?" Tassie asked.

Margot threw a smile at Tassie over her shoulder as she led the way into the living room. "All the time. I'm a lot stronger than I look, you know. Years of gardening will do that to you."

It wasn't until Margot closed the door behind Tassie and Baxter with an invitation to stop by any time that the woman's seemingly offhanded comment about killing Conrad suddenly echoed in her mind. She looked at Baxter, wrestling with the unsettling possibility that the sweet woman she'd spent the past thirty minutes with might be a murderer.

"Are you thinking what I'm thinking?" she asked her dog.

Baxter gave her a knowing look that Tassie took to be a yes.

"I agree that it's difficult to imagine someone like Margot killing anyone," she said. "Heck, I didn't even think she'd have the strength to pick up that model ship and hit Conrad over the head with it. But she did admit that she picks up those heavy bags of birdseed all the time. And she didn't like Conrad, that's for sure."

Tassie crouched down to scratch Baxter behind the ears.

"Perhaps most importantly, it would explain why Margot was so quick to tell Detective Sterling that she saw Sara fighting with Conrad. If Margot did murder Conrad, it makes sense she'd want to point the police in someone else's direction."

Tassie sighed. "But I can't go to Detective Sterling and insist he arrest Margot simply because she can pick up a twenty-five-pound bag of birdseed and didn't like Conrad any more than anyone else. Especially since I might be all wrong about her. For now, we'll just have to keep her on the list of suspects."

As she led Baxter off the porch, Tassie realized that solving Conrad's murder might be more complicated than she realized. Especially now that her main witness had just become a suspect.

Chapter 8

"Since we didn't get to go yesterday, want to go the dog park for a little while before we go back to the shop?" Tassie asked Baxter.

Figuring the answer to that question was always yes since her fur baby loved the dog park, Tassie started in that direction. The sun would be setting in about an hour or so, but they could squeeze in a little playtime and still get back to the shop before then.

Baxter, however, had other ideas. Instead of falling into step beside her, he stood where he was, little legs spread wide, letting her know he had no intention of going anywhere. Much to her chagrin, he was focused on Conrad's house.

Like yesterday.

Tassie wasn't sure exactly where this was going but she already didn't like it.

"What?" she demanded.

Baxter looked at Tassie, then at Conrad's house again before turning back to her.

"No way. We aren't doing this again," she said. "Finding one dead body was enough, thank you very much. Let's go."

But instead of going the way she wanted to go, Baxter let out a little yip, then stepped off the sidewalk and started toward Conrad's house. He was always a very compliant little dog, so if he wanted to check out Conrad's house, there must be a good reason. Maybe he'd sniffed out a clue.

"Okay," she said, letting Baxter lead her across the lawn. "But we really shouldn't be trespassing on private property, you know."

Then again, was it still trespassing if Conrad was dead?

Tassie expected Baxter to follow his nose directly up onto the porch and right to the crime scene tape strung across the door to keep people out. But he surprised her by leading her around the house and into the backyard.

O-kay.

"Where are we going, baby?" she asked.

Hopefully, not on a wild squirrel chase.

The trees at the edge of the clearing dappled the yard in shadows and Tassie let out a little shudder. It was creepy back here. And while it wasn't anywhere near overgrown, it wasn't going to win any awards in *Better Homes & Gardens* either.

Perhaps that's why Conrad was planting those golden glows. Maybe even he thought the yard needed sprucing up.

As for Baxter, he clearly didn't care what the yard looked like. He was more interested in sniffing every square inch of grass.

"Okay, Baxter," she said, glancing over her shoulder at the house looming behind them in the shadows. "Let's make this quick. We don't want someone finding us back here and calling the police."

Tassie groaned inwardly. She could only imagine what Detective Sterling would say. Probably something about them messing up an active crime scene. And admittedly looking more gorgeous than he had a right to be while he did.

Out ahead of her, Baxter snuffled at a part of the yard with fresh dirt, then pawed at it. Was that where Conrad had planted the golden glow?

Afraid Baxter might try to eat the seeds if he managed to dig them up, Tassie hurried forward, opening her mouth to call out his name. But before she could, Baxter stopped what he was doing and looked at her, letting out a sharp bark.

"What's so interesting?" Tassie asked.

She moved closer so she could see what he was looking at. All she saw was dirt and more dirt.

Baxter must have realized she was clueless because he pawed at the soil again, revealing something that looked suspiciously like a human finger.

Sure it couldn't possibly be that, she crouched down to get a better view.

And almost fell on her butt when she realized she was right.

It *was* a human finger. A man's if she wasn't mistaken.

Yikes!

What was a finger doing in Conrad's backyard?

Maybe a bird had picked it up somewhere else and dropped it here. That could happen, right? And lots of birds hung around Margot's house with those feeders out there and all.

Even so, that seemed a little far-fetched. Where would a bird find a finger?

Tassie looked at the finger again. At the moment, maybe more important than how it got there was whether it was still attached to a hand or not.

She didn't want to touch the thing—or contaminate the crime scene, if that's what it turned out to be—to find out though. She didn't want Baxter digging around it anymore either.

Thanks to all the trees, there were a lot of twigs on the ground. Picking the sturdiest looking one she could find, she gently brushed away some more dirt to reveal another finger, followed by another.

Then a hand.

And the sleeve of what looked like a windbreaker.

Tassie dropped the twig. She'd seen enough.

Fishing her phone out of her crossbody bag, she dialed 9-1-1, then waited.

"9-1-1, what's your emergency?"

"Lucy, it's Tassie," she said. "I found another dead body."

"What?! Where?"

"Buried in Conrad's backyard."

Lucy was silent for a moment, as if she was too stunned to say anything. Then she mumbled something Tassie couldn't understand, her voice muffled, like she had her hand over the phone while she was talking to someone.

"Stay there, Tassie," she finally said. "Jack's on his way now."

Sighing, Tassie hung up and looked at Baxter. "So, I guess we're stuck here until Detective Sterling shows up."

In a shadow-covered backyard that seemed even creepier now that she'd found a dead body.

She wrapped her arms around her and took a few steps back. Baxter sat beside her, his attention fixed on the dirt-encrusted hand. Tassie would rather have looked anywhere but at that, and yet, her gaze kept wandering back there.

"So, who do you think this poor guy is, Baxter?"

He turned his head to look up at her then went back to staring at the lifeless hand in the dirt.

"Yeah, I have no idea either," she said. "And who killed him and buried him here? Do you think it was Conrad? That makes sense, I suppose. If anyone else did it, Conrad surely would have noticed the body and called the police. Unless he was protecting whoever did it and that person ended up killing him because they were afraid he'd change his mind and turn them in."

She sighed. This was getting more convoluted by the minute.

Tassie was still trying to fit together the few pieces she had when Detective Sterling showed up. He was accompanied by Henry, the same uniformed officer that was with him yesterday, as well as the coroner and his assistant. Baxter immediately wagged his tail in greeting as the detective walked over to them.

"Baxter," he said, leaning down to give him a pet on the head before straightening up again and giving her a pointed look. "You seem to have a knack for finding dead bodies, Ms. Drake. That's two in as many days."

Lucky her.

"Trust me, it wasn't on my list of things to do today," she said dryly.

"Uh huh." His gaze was sharp as he eyed her. "Care to show me where the body is?"

Tassie considered staying where she was and pointing it out but decided it would probably be easier to show him. Especially since Baxter was already leading the way.

"It's over here," she said as the detective fell into step beside them.

When they reached the area near the tree line, Tassie hung back a little with Baxter, who seemed extremely interested in what Detective Sterling was doing as the man crouched down to get a closer look. The coroner joined him, brushing away the dirt to reveal more of the body until he'd unearthed all of it. The body hadn't been buried very deep.

"I'll know more when we get the body back to the morgue, but I'd say whoever this guy is, he's been here about three weeks."

Detective Sterling looked at Tassie. "Recognize him?"

She'd been trying to avoid looking at the man's face, but at the question, she forced herself to take a quick peek, then glanced away. The sight wasn't as grotesque as she imagined. Other than the fact that his skin was an ashen color and there were still traces of dirt on it, he might have been sleeping.

Only he wasn't.

She shuddered.

"No," she said. "I've never seen him before."

The detective said something to the uniformed officer she didn't catch, then walked over to her.

"I didn't see a car out front. I'm assuming that you walked down here from your shop?" he said.

She nodded. "Yes."

"Come on. It'll be dark soon. I'll give you and Baxter a ride."

"Um." Tassie glanced at Baxter to see him gazing up at her with a doggy smile. Apparently, he was all about getting a lift back to Pupcakes. She looked at Detective Sterling. "Okay. Thanks."

Picking up Baxter, she fell into step beside the detective. His SUV was parked in the driveway, and he opened the passenger door for her. Climbing in, she put on her seatbelt then settled Baxter on her lap and waited for Detective Sterling to join her. She noticed he had a safety divider between the back seat and cargo area for his dog. She'd have to remember to ask him about his pooch.

He glanced at her as he turned onto the street. "So, what exactly were you doing in Conrad's backyard?"

Tassie didn't say anything. She should have had an answer ready for that.

"Would you believe me if I said Baxter and I were out for a walk, and he chased a squirrel back there?" she asked.

"Maybe. If it were true." He gave her another quick look. "But something tells me it isn't that simple."

Tassie sighed. It figured he'd see through that. She contemplated trying to come up with a more creative tale, but in the end, honesty finally won out. "I was here to talk to Margot Henderson."

He frowned. "The neighbor who saw Sara fighting with Conrad?"

"Yeah. I wanted to see if she saw anyone else around besides Sara."

The frown turned into a scowl. "You don't think I asked her that same thing when I spoke to her yesterday?"

"Well, yeah." He'd obviously been a cop for a while so Tassie suspected he was good at his job. Even if he did believe her friend was a murderer. "But some people are more comfortable talking to a civilian than to the police."

He seemed to consider that. "And did she tell you anything she didn't tell me?"

She gave him a sweet smile in the growing darkness. "Since I don't know exactly what Margot told you, I can't precisely say. Unless you want to fill me in, of course."

Detective Sterling slanted her a hard look.

"I'll take that as a no," Tassie said.

Sighing, she quickly recounted the conversation she'd had with Margot.

"You know," Tassie added, "it's quite possible that she could have killed Conrad."

He pulled up to the cobblestone sidewalk in front of Pupcakes and put the SUV in park before turning to give her a dubious look. "You're telling me that nice older woman bludgeoned a man?"

"No. I'm saying she *could* have. She told me that she can pick up a twenty-five-pound bag of bird seed, so she certainly has the muscle to do it." Tassie shrugged. "On top of that, she didn't like Conrad, so she had motive."

He lifted a brow. "Using that logic, then nearly everyone in Bluewater Bay is a suspect—including you."

She did a double take. "Me?"

The detective was the one to shrug this time. "You admitted that you didn't like the victim."

Tassie wrapped her arm around Baxter a little tighter as he cuddled against her. "But I called the police. I wouldn't have done that if I killed Conrad. That makes no sense."

"Maybe you were trying to deflect suspicion from yourself."

"That's ridiculous!"

So was sitting in his SUV listening to this. But she couldn't get out until she convinced him that she wasn't the murderer. She wanted him to stop focusing on Sara being the killer but not so he could turn his sights on her instead.

"In fact," he continued, "if I wanted to, I could make the assumption that finding two dead bodies in as many days puts you at the top of the list of suspects for both murders."

Tassie stared at him in disbelief, mouth open. How had this conversation gone sideways so fast?

She was about to reach for the door handle so she and Baxter could make a run for it before Detective Sterling knew what had happened when he spoke.

"I said that I *could* make that assumption if I wanted to."

She eyed him warily. "So, you *don't* think I murdered Conrad or the guy I found today?"

Were all detectives this confusing or just him?

His mouth edged up. "No, I don't think you killed either of them. I just wanted to show you how dangerous it is to start accusing people of murder. I know you're trying to help your friend, but stay out of this and let me do the investigating, okay?"

Tassie considered that. She was pretty sure that blatantly lying to an officer of the law was a crime, so she went with something as close to the truth as she could.

"I'll think about it."

She expected some pushback on that, but instead, he shook his head in obvious resignation.

Stepping out of the SUV, Detective Sterling came around to her side and opened the door.

"Keep your mom out of trouble, Baxter," he said when they'd climbed out.

Huh! Little did he know that Baxter was her partner in crime—so to speak.

"Thanks for the ride, Detective," Tassie said.

"Anytime." He flashed her a smile. "Though maybe next time we could do it without you stumbling on a crime scene."

Tassie couldn't help laughing. She'd like that. "Deal."

Although considering her track record the past couple days, maybe she shouldn't be so quick to promise something like that. She wouldn't mind spending time with him outside of work though.

"Then it's a date," he said. "Good night, Ms. Drake."

A date? Had they set something up that she didn't remember? Maybe it was just a figure of speech. Bluewater Bay was a small town, so they'd almost certainly run into each other.

"Good night, Detective."

Abby practically pounced on Tassie the moment she walked into Pupcakes. The delightful scents of peanut butter and cinnamon immediately wrapped around her like a warm hug.

"Who was *that?*" her sister asked, curiously peeking around her to look out the big picture window.

Tassie took off Baxter's leash and harness, then set him on the floor so he could visit with Finn. Baxter and

Abby's Dachshund touched their noses to each other in greeting, then pranced to the breakroom.

"That was Detective Sterling," Tassie said, heading in that direction too.

Abby followed. "Oh! He *is* good looking. Tall, too.

Tassie smiled but didn't say anything.

"Wait," her sister said. "Why were you with him? I thought you were going to talk to Conrad's neighbor."

"I did."

Tassie told her sister about her conversation with Margot and finding the body buried in Conrad's backyard.

Abby made a face. "You're becoming a real murder magnet, you know that?"

Ugh, she hoped not. She definitely didn't want this becoming a regular thing. Stumbling upon two dead bodies in two days was enough for her.

"So, how does this second murder connect to Conrad's death, if at all?" Abby asked.

"I think this is actually the first murder since the man was killed before Conrad," Tassie corrected. "While I'm not sure it has anything to do with it, I find it difficult to believe it's a coincidence that he was buried in Conrad's backyard. And if the two murders are connected, then that could help clear Sara's name."

Now, Tassie simply had to discover that connection.

Chapter 9

The third time must have been the charm, Tassie thought, because she and Baxter finally made it to the dog park the next day. Pupcakes had been busy in the morning, so she hadn't been able to get away until after the rush. Not that she was complaining. All that business helped keep Baxter and Finn in toys and kibble. Not to mention made the dogs in Bluewater Bay happy with all those tasty baked goods.

But as much as she loved the shop, it was nice to get away for a while so she could think about how to approach the next step in her investigation. Since she didn't know who the dead man in the backyard was because the police hadn't released his name to the media yet, she couldn't connect him to Conrad. While Bluewater Bay might be a small town, they had a very good newspaper that updated their social media with all the important stories. She knew they hadn't reported anything yet because she'd constantly been checking her phone since they'd gotten to the dog park.

Tassie glanced up from her phone to see what Baxter was up to. The park was quite big with lots of doggy playground equipment including agility ramps, hoops to jump through, and tunnels to crawl around in. As for the pet parents like her, there were comfortable benches and cute picnic tables. Regardless of how spacious it was, thankfully, her baby never ventured far from where she was. Right now, he was playing on the agility ramps a few feet away from where she sat while he still kept an eye out for the occasional bold—and reckless—squirrel that sometimes ventured into the park.

She was smiling at how cute Baxter looked in his little plaid jacket when she caught sight of movement over by the entrance to the park. For safety purposes, it was a double gate system, kind of like an airlock on a spaceship. When you came in, you closed the gate to the outside, then opened the gate to the park itself. At this time of day, people came in and out regularly, but she was a little surprised to see the man who was quickly becoming her favorite detective navigating the doors.

And he was here with his dog—a gorgeous black Lab mix!

Once they were inside the fenced-in area, Detective Sterling unhooked the leash so his dog could explore the park, but for the moment, the pup seemed more interested in checking everything out from right where he was.

Over on the agility ramp, Baxter stopped what he was doing and regarded the detective and his dog curiously, ears perked and tail wagging.

Even though Detective Sterling probably already saw her—especially since they were the only ones in the park at the moment—Tassie lifted her arm and waved anyway. He waved back and headed her way, his dog at his side. Baxter eagerly jumped off the ramp to greet them, wanting to be friends with the bigger dog.

"This is Gus," he said with a grin, running his hand up and down the Lab's back, then giving him a pat.

"Hello, Gus," she said, offering her hand so he could give it a sniff and decide if he wanted her to pet him. When he happily nudged her fingers, she caressed his floppy ears with a smile. "Nice to meet you."

With the introductions out of the way, Baxter and Gus went off on their own to play, leaving her and the detective to their own devices.

"Detective," she said as he sat down beside her.

He grinned again. "Jack, please."

She returned his smile. "Jack."

He made a show of looking around the dog park.

Wondering what he was searching for, she looked around too.

"What are you doing?" she asked.

He turned back to her. "Checking for dead bodies."

She blinked. "What?"

His mouth twitched. "Well, there were dead bodies around the previous two times we met, so I just wanted to make sure."

"And?"

"Not a dead body in sight."

Tassie couldn't help but laugh. "Thank goodness for that. Although..."

Jack's brow lifted above the top of his dark sunglasses.

"Since we're on the subject," she said, "did you figure out who the guy is that was buried in Conrad's backyard? And before you say you can't share that information, I'm pretty sure you'll be releasing his name to the media soon enough anyway, so..."

He regarded her for a moment before letting out a sigh. "You should have been a reporter, you know that? The victim's name is Oliver Bolton. He was about Conrad's age."

She repeated the name over in her head, trying to see if she recognized it. "He doesn't sound familiar."

"Probably because he didn't live in Bluewater Bay. He's from Southport."

That explained it. Southport was to the west of them, and much smaller in population than Bluewater Bay. Tassie's sister had dated a guy who lived there a few years ago, and while Tassie had driven past the town a lot of times on the way to somewhere else, she'd never been there herself.

"Do you know what he was doing in Bluewater Bay?" she asked.

"According to his social media pages, he did a lot of deep-sea fishing with Conrad, so they were almost certainly friends. The last photo Oliver posted was of the two of them on a boat a few weeks ago."

She thought a moment. "That's when the coroner said Oliver was murdered. So Conrad must have been the one who killed him and buried him in the backyard."

Something Sara said yesterday popped into Tassie's head about Conrad not wanting her and Roxie in the yard when she'd stopped by his house a few weeks ago with Tristan. Conrad had probably just buried the body and didn't want Sara's dog sniffing around. So much for planting those golden glow he'd told Margot about.

"It seems that way," Jack agreed. "We just haven't figured out why he did it. I'm going over to Southport later to see what I can find out about Oliver."

Why Conrad had killed Oliver was something Tassie was fine with letting Jack and his fellow police officers figure out. She was more concerned with other things. Like whether it was possible someone close to Oliver learned what Conrad had done and killed him in a fit of rage.

But when she mentioned that theory to Jack, he shook his head.

"Oliver didn't have any family in Maine or anywhere else. His parents were killed in a car accident when he was a kid, and he grew up in the foster care system."

"Drats," Tassie muttered. "I was hoping to give you another suspect for Conrad's murder besides Sara."

Jack turned his head to gaze at Baxter and Gus, watching as they playfully chased each other around. "You seem very sure she didn't do it."

"I am," Tassie said.

Jack considered that. "Sometimes you think you know someone and then they end up doing something you never thought they were capable of."

She regarded him thoughtfully. "You sound like you're speaking from experience."

He let out a little snort in answer but didn't say anything.

She'd take that as a yes. Even though she was curious, she forced herself not to pry. At least until she knew him a little better. Time to change to a less delicate topic.

"It looks like our fur babies are becoming fast friends," Tassie said, laughing as Baxter and Gus took turns running through the tunnel.

Jack chuckled, his gaze lingering on the joyful chaos that was happy barks, wagging tails, and bounding paws. "Yeah, they are."

The breeze coming off the bay teased Tassie's hair, and she reached up to tuck it behind her ear. "Is Gus a rescue?"

"Yeah," Jack said. "I adopted him a little while before moving here."

"From Albany, right?" she said, then gave him a sheepish look. "Lucy mentioned you were from New York."

"Of course, she did." He shook his head with a chuckle. "Yeah, I was a cop in Albany. Born and raised there actually."

"What made you move to Bluewater Bay?" she asked.

Jack didn't answer right away, instead turning his attention back to their pups. He was silent for so long she thought he wasn't going to say anything, but then he finally spoke.

"Girlfriend trouble. I found out that she was cheating on me with my partner."

Ouch. That was worse than the toad cheating on her with a waitress.

"Oh…wow," Tassie said. "I'm sorry about that."

And, if she was being honest, kind of surprised. What woman in her right mind would cheat on a man like him?

"Thanks." His mouth edged up. "Luckily, Bluewater Bay needed a detective at the same time that I was looking for a change of scenery."

She returned his smile. "And what do you think of our small town in Maine?"

"I like it." He looked at her and his grin broadened. "A lot."

Tassie felt her pulse skip a beat as she realized Jack wasn't talking about Bluewater Bay—at least not entirely. She didn't know how long they sat there gazing at each other like that, but they might still be doing so if Baxter and Gus hadn't run over to them. The former jumped into her lap and licked her face while the latter hopped up to put his paws on Jack's leg and affectionately nuzzled his hand.

Laughing, she hugged Baxter close as Jack ruffled Gus's ears with a deep chuckle.

"Although," he said after a moment, "I have to admit, I didn't expect to have to investigate so many murders in a town like this."

She ran her hand over Baxter's fur with a sigh. "It's kind of ironic in a way. Everyone always think people are so lucky when they win the lottery, but it obviously wasn't lucky for Conrad. I mean, first, he kills a man and buries the guy in his backyard, and then, a few weeks later, someone murders him. That's got to be the opposite of lucky." She frowned as a thought occurred to her. "You did know Conrad won millions in the lottery a few weeks ago, right?"

Jack nodded. "The chief told me about it. That's another angle to the murder that I'm investigating."

Tassie's ears perked up. "So you don't think Sara killed Conrad then?"

"I'm still considering other suspects, if that's what you're asking."

Yes!

"Money is a great motive for murder," she said excitedly. "At least it is on TV shows."

He regarded her from behind his sunglasses, a thoughtful expression on his face. "I know you're only trying to help Sara and I also know that I'd be wasting my breath if I ask you to give up trying to clear her name because something tells me you're going to do it anyway. So, I'll make a deal with you."

She eyed him warily. "O-kay."

"I won't ask you to stop playing Miss Marple if you promise to be careful and call me if you even suspect anyone. I don't want you putting yourself in danger trying to get a confession from someone."

Tassie stared. He'd just told her that he wouldn't interfere with her investigating and all she could do was focus on one thing. "You read Agatha Christie?"

Not that a man couldn't read cozy mysteries, but considering Jack was a cop, something told her that he wasn't all that into books featuring amateur detectives.

He chuckled. "My grandmother does. I'm more of a Lee Child guy."

"Right. That makes more sense."

"So, are we in agreement?"

"Yes." She nodded. There was no need to get on the bad side of the detective working the investigation, after all. Particularly when she needed him on her side. "I can do that."

"Good." He pulled out his phone and glanced at the time. "I need to get back to the station. I'm glad Gus and I ran into you and Baxter."

Tassie smiled. "Me, too. You should come by Pupcakes sometime. You know, so you can pick up some baked goodies for Gus."

"I'll do that." Jack flashed her a grin, then put Gus on his leash. "Okay, boy. Let's get back to work."

Tassie watched them go, returning the wave Jack gave her as he and his dog left the enclosure and headed for the adjacent parking lot. She should be getting back to work, too. Not only did she have doggy treats to bake, but she still had a murderer to catch.

Chapter 10

"Sorry we're late getting back," Tassie told her sister when they walked into Pupcakes. "Baxter and I ran into Jack and his fur baby at the dog park."

While not as busy as it was earlier in the day, there were a few regulars and their dogs in the shop picking out treats and toys. Tassie returned their smiles and waves as she and Baxter made their way to the cash register.

On the other side of the counter, Abby frowned. "Jack?"

"Detective Sterling," Tassie explained as she helped Baxter out of his harness and jacket.

Her sister grinned. "So he's *Jack* now, is he? Next, you'll be picking out wedding invitations."

"Ha. Ha. Very funny," Tassie said. "It's just easier to investigate Conrad's murder when you're friends with the detective working the case."

"Especially one who's such a hottie."

"See how that works?" Tassie teased. "I didn't even have to manufacture a reason to talk to him. Unlike a sister of mine who has a thing for a certain dog psychologist."

"Very funny."

Abby wasn't wrong about Jack being a hottie though. But before Tassie could insist that how attractive Jack was didn't factor into things at all—which they didn't because she wasn't that shallow—the bell above the door tinkled merrily, announcing a customer. She turned to see a woman coming into the shop with her Corgi. Petite with short, dark hair touched with gray, and big, round glasses, Estelle Nichols worked at the Bluewater Bay Historical Society and had been coming into Pupcakes ever since the first day they'd opened shop.

"Good afternoon, ladies," she said with a smile. "I'm here to pick up the cake I ordered for Snickers' birthday."

"It's in the back," Abby said, returning her smile. "I'll go get it for you."

Tassie leaned down to give the Corgi a pat even as Baxter pranced over to greet him. "Hey there, Snickers."

Snickers wiggled his butt in greeting.

Laughing, Tassie straightened, catching sight of the handmade soap that Estelle had placed on the counter while she waited. Packed in the clear bag with a sticker featuring Sara's fancy logo, the delightful scent filled the air.

"Is that honeysuckle strawberry?" Tassie asked. "That's my absolute favorite soap that Sara makes."

Estelle smiled. "Yes. It's one of my favorites too. I already have way more of Sara's soaps than I'll ever need, but I wanted to show my support, so I purchased more when I stopped by to see her today. Did you know that she had some people call to cancel the soaps they'd custom ordered after hearing she'd been arrested?" She made a small tsking sound. "I'm just sick over the thought of that poor girl going to jail. As her friend, I'm sure you are as well. I can't imagine what the police were thinking arresting her for murdering that creep, Conrad. I don't believe she did it."

"I don't believe she did either." Tassie sighed. "The whole thing is a mess."

Estelle glanced down at Snickers. Her pooch was eyeing the various frosted treats in the glass display under the counter. "Trust me, there are a lot of people in this town who wouldn't have minded seeing Conrad six feet under."

"Oh?" Tassie leaned one hip against the counter, trying to appear casual even though her antennas were fully up and alert. "Anyone in particular?"

"His ex-wife, for one. Belinda despised him."

"Really?" Tassie said.

Estelle nodded. "Oh, yes. They've been divorced for more than a decade, but you'd never know it from the way Belinda talked whenever she mentioned Conrad. Far be it from me to gossip but..."

"Of course," Tassie murmured.

Was it really gossip if what you were saying was helping with a murder investigation?

Estelle looked around the shop like she was afraid someone might be listening to their conversation, then lowered her voice conspiratorially.

"More than one person told me that they overheard Belinda on several occasions say that Conrad made her so furious she could kill him."

Tassie glanced over to see Baxter looking up at her. She couldn't be entirely sure, of course, but she got the feeling he was thinking the same thing she was. Belinda could be the murderer!

"Then again, Conrad's son didn't much care for him either," Estelle continued. "When Tristan worked at the historical society during the summer between his freshman and sophomore year of high school, Conrad used to come in all the time, and I'd hear the two of them fighting."

"Do you know what they were fighting about?"

She let out a sigh. "Conrad wanted his son to work with him at his charter fishing business, but Tristan never had any interest in it. Conrad thought he was too much of a mama's boy. I guess he believed deep sea fishing would toughen Tristan up or something ridiculous like that, but badgering his son only drove more of a wedge between them. I overheard Tristan telling his friends more than once that he wished his father was out of his life for good."

Tassie winced. That was kind of harsh regardless of who your father was. Then again, this was Conrad they were talking about. She couldn't imagine growing up with him as a parent.

"That was a long time ago," Tassie said. "Do you think Tristan still harbored enough resentment against his father to murder him all these years later?"

Estelle lifted a shoulder in a shrug. "I haven't seen much of Tristan since he was a teenager, so I really couldn't say. I'd hate to see him go to jail any more than Sara though." She pursed her lips a moment, thinking. "Honestly, I wouldn't be surprised if Conrad's business partner was the one who killed him."

Of course, there was *another* suspect. Because it couldn't be that easy.

"They weren't the best of friends I take it?" she asked.

"They were until Conrad won the lottery," Estelle said.

Tassie had always thought that everyone wanted to be your bestie if you won all that money. Apparently not.

"What happened?" Tassie asked.

"Good old-fashioned jealousy and resentment, I suppose," Estelle said. "When you win millions, your friends expect you to share some of it, you know."

"I suppose. But Conrad didn't seem like the generous type," Tassie said.

"He wasn't," Estelle agreed, smiling as Abby joined them.

Abby placed a small cake box on the counter and lifted the lid to show Estelle the tiny peanut butter carrot cake decorated with *Happy Birthday Snickers!* in yogurt frosting.

"It's perfect!" Estelle declared. "Snickers will love it."

Closing the box, Estelle fished her credit card out of her purse and paid for the cake, then gently put her hand on Tassie's arm.

"Don't worry about Sara," she said. "The police will find the real murderer. I'm sure of it. Oh, and I'll tag Pupcakes on social media when I post pictures of Snickers' birthday party."

Tassie smiled and thanked her.

"You didn't tell her that you're investigating the murder, did you?" Abby asked as soon as Estele and Snickers left. "I love her, but you know how she likes to gossip. Everyone in town will hear about it."

"No, I didn't tell her," Tassie said with a laugh. "She doesn't believe Sara did it either so we were simply talking about who she thinks could have killed Conrad. I already had his ex-wife and business partner on the list, but Estelle made a good argument for his son so I'm going to add him to the suspects as well."

Abby frowned. "I thought you said that Sara's lawyer is a friend of Tristan's."

"He is." Tassie shrugged. "He also wants her to take a plea deal for a lesser sentence, which is exactly something a lawyer who's friends with the real murderer might advise his client to do."

Her sister considered that. "And risk getting himself disbarred? I don't know about that, but I suppose you could be right. So, which suspect are you going to talk to first?"

Tassie didn't even have to think about it. "The ex-wife."

"Well then, you're in luck." Abby picked up a piece of paper from the counter and held it out to her. "Conrad's ex stopped by when you were at the dog park and asked if she could leave this here. It's bring-your-dog-to-the-gallery night."

Tassie scanned the colorful flier for Belinda's gallery, Unchartered Art. She was all about any business that was dog friendly and holding an event like this at an art gallery was genius. While she'd be completely unbiased in her investigation, part of Tassie was already hoping Belinda didn't turn out to be the murderer. Anyone who loved dogs was okay in her eyes.

Picking up Baxter, Tassie cradled him in one arm while she showed him the flier with her free hand. "Looks like you and I are going to bring-your-dog-to-the-gallery night to question the next suspect on our list."

Chapter 11

"Would you mind if I ran over to check on Sara real quick?" Tassie asked her sister an hour later. "Estelle said that a lot of people canceled custom orders for soap after hearing she'd gotten arrested, and I want to check to see how she's doing."

Abby nodded. "Yeah, of course. Go ahead. Tell her I said hi."

"I will."

Like everything in Bluewater Bay, it didn't take long to get from Pupcakes to Sara's. Tassie parked her SUV in a visitor's space then attached Baxter's leash to his harness and led him upstairs to Sara's apartment. Her friend answered the door right away, Roxie right beside her.

"Tassie! Hi. Come in."

Tassie took her up on the offer, unhooking Baxter's leash so he and Roxie could hang out.

"Do you want something to drink?" Sara asked over her shoulder as she led the way into the living room. "I haven't had the energy to go grocery shopping since…well…I got arrested, but I think I still have some bottled water and iced tea. Or I could make hot tea if you want?"

"I'm good, thanks." Tassie glanced over at the craft table Sara used to make her candles, unable to help smiling at the adorable molds for the teddy bear soaps. "These are so cute! Are these for the baby shower?"

Sara stopped to run her hand over the silicone molds, giving her a half-hearted smile. "Uh-huh. I thought I should make them now since I'll probably be in jail by then."

Tassie turned to look at Sara, her heart aching at the tears welling in her friend's eyes. Teddy bear molds forgotten, she quickly moved to hug Sara.

"Hey, it's going to be okay," she said. "You *aren't* going to be in jail."

Sara sniffed as she returned her embrace. "You don't know that."

"Yes, I do," Tassie said firmly, stepping back to give Sara a reassuring look. "In fact, I talked to Detective Sterling earlier and he said that he's not convinced you murdered Conrad."

Well, that wasn't *exactly* what he said. But it was close enough, Tassie thought, ignoring the side eye Baxter gave her.

Sara's eyes lit up, hope reflected there. "Does he have any suspects yet?"

"Not yet but he's working on it. And so am I," Tassie said. "As a matter of fact, I'm going to talk to Conrad's ex-wife tonight. She's having a bring-your-dog-to-the-gallery event so I figured it'd be the perfect opportunity."

Her friend frowned, a horrified look on her face. "You don't think Tristan's mother killed Conrad, do you?"

Drats. Considering Sara was dating Conrad's son, maybe she shouldn't have said that.

"I just want to see if she knows who might have done it," Tassie said, choosing her words carefully.

"Oh." She nodded thoughtfully, leading the way over to the couch. "That makes sense. I know Tristan didn't like his father very much but he's really close with his mother. I don't even want to think how devastated he'd be if Belinda went to jail for Conrad's murder."

Devastated enough to instead let Sara go to prison for a crime she didn't commit if it meant keeping his mother out of jail? That was a chilling thought.

Tassie sat down on the couch beside her. "How are things going with you and Tristan?"

Sara's lips curved. "Tristan has been my rock. I don't think I'd be keeping it together right now if it weren't for him."

"I'm glad."

"I only wish I could get him to stop blaming himself for me getting arrested," Sara added. "He thinks that if he was with me when I took Roxie to the dog park the other day then I wouldn't have gotten into a fight with his father."

Huh.

Tassie chewed the inside of her lip thoughtfully. "Why didn't he go with you?"

"He was at his place working on a new song."

"Was he with the guys in his band?"

Sara shook her head. "No. Tristan likes to be by himself when he writes songs."

So, he didn't have an alibi for the time of his father's murder. Well, that was an interesting tidbit of information to file away for later.

"How are your parents handling this whole thing?" Tassie asked.

Sara made a face. "Mom and Dad left to go on a Caribbean cruise a few days before Conrad was murdered and won't be back until Sunday, so they don't know yet."

That explained why Sara called her to babysit Roxie the night she was arrested instead of her parents.

She reached out to give Sara's hand a squeeze. "Well, with any luck, we'll figure out who really killed Conrad by the time they get home."

Tassie hoped.

Chapter 12

Unchartered Art was located a few blocks down the street from Pupcakes, nestled between a jeweler called The Jewelry Box and a microbrewery named Coastal Aleworks. Like the fine jewelry store beside it, Unchartered Art had set up shop in a restored nineteenth-century home. In addition to the big abstract sculptures lining the walkway, there was a picture window to the left of the door featuring a beautiful framed oil painting of a seascape on an easel.

When they stepped inside, Tassie was surprised to see how crowded the gallery was. She recognized almost everyone and their dogs since most all of them were regular customers at Pupcakes. She smiled and waved at them even as she casually looked around for Jack in the big room off the entryway. Probably originally a living area, it was now home to a few sculptures on pedestals and framed paintings that hung on the walls. She'd hoped that he and Gus might be in attendance, but maybe gallery events weren't his thing. Then again, the converted home boasted several rooms, so maybe she'd run into her crush in one of them.

"I didn't know you girls would be here!"

Tassie turned to see Estelle coming their way, Snickers at her heels. She smiled at the woman even though she was cringing on the inside. She really didn't want an audience when she spoke to Belinda. Especially if that audience included someone as prone to gossip as Estelle.

"It was a spur-of-the-moment kind of thing," Tassie said. "Belinda dropped off the fliers this afternoon and it looked like a fun outing, so here we are."

"I personally think this event is genius! I'm considering stealing the idea and doing something like this at the historical society." Estelle lowered her voice. "Though the timing of it is a little suspect, don't you think? Belinda's ex just got murdered the other day and she's hosting a party?"

"Maybe that's exactly why she *is* hosting it," Lucy pointed out.

Which was Tassie's cue to find Belinda so she could interrogate her. But first she had to get away from Estelle.

"Baxter sees a dog he knows, so we're going to say hello," Tassie said, giving Abby and Lucy a pointed look, hoping they'd figure out what she was trying to tell them.

Thankfully, her sister and her friend were quick on the uptake. Both of them immediately engaged Estelle in conversation about the current quilt exhibit at the historical society. Mouthing a quick "thank you," Tassie extricated herself from the group and began slowly making her way through the various rooms, looking for Belinda. Unfortunately, she was nowhere to be seen. The woman was hosting the event. Shouldn't she be around here somewhere?

It wasn't a complete bust. Yet, anyway. Baxter enjoyed wandering from room to room, seeing familiar canine faces and meeting dogs that were new to him while Tassie made small talk with their human counterparts, catching up with the people she knew and introducing herself to those she didn't.

"Tassie, hey! I wondered if you'd be here."

Tassie turned to see Irene Bartlett behind her with Luna, her Shar Pei mix, whom Baxter was already happily greeting.

"Irene!" she said, giving the other woman a warm hug. "How are you? I haven't seen you at Pupcakes in a while."

Irene pushed her wavy strawberry blonde hair over her shoulder. "I know. I've been busy coming up with the perfect recipes for the baking contest I'm competing in."

Oh, gosh! She'd been so preoccupied with this murder investigation, Tassie had forgotten all about the upcoming baking competition the Dessert Channel was coming to Bluewater Bay to film in a few weeks.

"Luckily, Graham always grabs a bag of treats for Luna whenever he stops by your shop to pick up something for his dog," Irene added. "I was going to text and ask if I should bring anything to Lucy's shower. Besides a gift, I mean. I was thinking about cupcakes. Everyone loves cupcakes."

Tassie blinked. "Um..."

Gwen was already making cupcakes. As in Irene's arch-rival, Gwen.

"And I already have the cutest decorations," Irene continued, practically bouncing up and down with excitement. "Lucy will love them! What do you think?"

"I think it's a great idea," Tassie said with a smile.

Not really. In fact, it was a terrible idea that was bound to blow up in Tassie's face when both Gwen and Irene showed up at the baby shower with cupcakes. But she didn't want to say no to Irene, so she'd deal with that then. Right now, she spotted Belinda moving into another room, a cell phone to her ear. Solving Conrad's murder was the priority at the moment.

"I just saw Belinda and want to tell her what a fantastic idea this event was," Tassie said to Irene. "Talk later?"

Irene grinned. "Definitely!"

As Tassie led Baxter around a group of people and their dogs in search of Belinda—where had she gone now?—she felt her fur baby's eyes on her.

"What was I supposed to do, tell her that she couldn't bring cupcakes?" Tassie asked. "You know what they say. You can never be too rich, too thin, or have too many cupcakes."

Baxter glanced at her again, his face dubious.

"Okay. No one ever says that," she muttered. "But they should."

Now, where did Belinda go?

Tassie caught sight of a flash of coppery red hair from the corner of her eye and quickly darted in that direction, exiting the room displaying watercolors of flowers and coming out into the hallway just in time to see Belinda disappearing into another room. Tassie quickly followed, only to slow her steps when she realized that Conrad's ex-wife was still on the phone. Tassie moved closer until she was right outside the door. It wasn't eavesdropping if you were trying to solve a murder.

"And you're sure that no one will find out I was behind this, right?" Belinda demanded. "Especially my son."

Behind what?

Conrad's murder maybe?

The garbled sound of a voice on the other end of the phone reached Tassie's ears. If only she could make out what the person was saying.

Belinda sighed. "All right. I'm just glad it's done. I'll Venmo you."

Not wanting to get caught standing there listening in on what was supposed to be a private conversation, Tassie scooped up Baxter and tiptoed as quickly down the hallway as she could, stopping in front of a watercolor of a little girl playing with her dog on the beach.

"That would look amazing in your shop," Belinda said from behind her.

Tassie silently thought so too until she saw the hefty price tag. Okay, maybe not. She turned to give Belinda a smile.

"This event is awesome," she said. "I'm so glad you came up with the idea."

Tall and willowy, Belinda elegantly shrugged one shoulder under her sage green cable-knit sweater. "I see so many people walk by with their dogs and stop to look in the windows but think they can't come inside. I considered putting up a sign saying *Dogs Welcome* but thought bring-your-dog-to-the-gallery night would be more fun. Since there's such a great turnout, I'm planning on making it a regular thing. Though next time, I'm going to have Pupcakes do the catering. It didn't occur to me until now that I should have had some treats for the pooches as well as their owners. You and your sister do catering, right?"

Now, Tassie felt even guiltier for thinking Belinda killed Conrad. But hey, the woman had just told someone on the phone that she was going to send them money for something she didn't want anyone to find out about. If that didn't scream hiring a contract killer to murder your ex, Tassie didn't know what did.

"We'd be glad to do the catering," Tassie said.

If Belinda wasn't in prison for murder, of course. Speaking of which.

"I'm sorry about Conrad," she offered.

Belinda stared at her in confusion for a moment, then waved a hand dismissively. "No need. Conrad and I got divorced years ago and haven't been on speaking terms since. Unless you count the regular arguments about custody and alimony when my son was younger."

"Oh," Tassie said, feigning surprise. "I knew you were divorced, but I didn't realize that things weren't amicable between the two of you."

She let out a delicate little snort. "I don't think there was a time when things were ever amicable between us, even when we were married. It just took me a little while to figure that out. I only wish Conrad would have played the lottery back then. Maybe I could have gotten more in the divorce settlement."

"Do you know who will inherit everything?" Tassie asked.

If money had been the motive for murder, then figuring out who would get all of those millions could narrow down the suspects.

"I'm hoping Conrad did the right thing and left all of it to my son, but since he and Tristan haven't spoken in years, I doubt it."

Huh. So Belinda didn't know that Tristan saw his father a few weeks before Conrad was murdered. She wondered why Tristan hadn't said anything to her. Was he worried she'd be angry? Or did he simply want to make sure she had plausible deniability because he'd intended to kill his father all along?

Whatever the reason, it wasn't Tassie's secret to tell. Besides, she was here to get information not supply it.

"Do you have any idea who could have murdered Conrad?" Tassie asked, trying to sound casual.

Belinda frowned. "The Bluewater Gazette said the police already arrested someone."

"They did. My friend, Sara," Tassie said.

"You know Sara?" Belinda asked in surprise. When Tassie nodded, she let out a sigh. "Then you know that she and Tristan are dating. The idea that sweet girl killed Conrad doesn't make sense to me. She doesn't even know him. My son is beside himself worrying that she's going to go to jail."

"So am I," Tassie admitted. "That's why I was hoping you might know who'd want to kill Conrad."

Belinda regarded her thoughtfully for a moment. "I haven't seen Conrad in a long time, but I'm sure there are probably a lot of people who wanted to kill him. I'm sorry about Sara being wrongly accused, I really am, but I can't help you. I have no idea who murdered Conrad." She gave Tassie a smile. "I should be getting back to the other guests."

Tassie nodded. "Of course. If you think of anything that might help, I do hope you'll mention it to the police."

"I'll do that."

Part of her wanted to tell Belinda that she'd overheard her phone conversation. Wanted to ask her outright if she'd hired someone to murder her ex-husband. But as Jack had pointed out, trying to get a confession from someone was dangerous, and she'd promised him that she wouldn't do that. Instead, she'd call him if she suspected anyone. At the moment, Belinda was on her list of suspects. For now, she needed to play it cool, go back to the party, and mingle.

Besides, Belinda owned the gallery. She wasn't going anywhere because she had no reason to think anyone suspected her.

Tassie started to follow Belinda back to the main part of the house when the woman stopped and turned to look at her.

"You might want to talk to Conrad's partner in his charter fishing business, David Campbell," she said. "If anyone might know what Conrad did to get himself killed, it would be David."

Tassie nodded and thanked her. This time, she didn't follow the other woman right away.

"What do you think, Baxter?" Tassie asked, looking at her fur baby. "Was Belinda genuinely trying to be helpful or was she offering up another suspect to deflect suspicion?"

Baxter licked the tip of her nose in answer.

"Yeah, I'm not sure either," Tassie said. "Hopefully, we'll get closer to an answer after we talk to some more suspects."

Sighing, she and Baxter made their way back to the main part of the house to find Lucy and her sister.

Chapter 13

"There he is!"

On the far side of Pupcakes, Abby looked up from the computer where she was doing inventory. "There who is?"

Tassie glanced over her shoulder at her sister. "Conrad's son. He just went into Hug in a Mug."

She hadn't been staring out the window specifically looking for Tristan the next morning, but it was lucky she'd been replacing the seasonal store display they kept there or she might not have seen him at all. Talking to him there would be much easier than trying to have a conversation at the club where his band played. Plus, she could bring Baxter to the coffee shop. The club, not so much.

Quickly placing the plush floppy-eared bunny and his doggy friend so they were leaning against the colorful Easter eggs of various sizes nestled among the silk plants, Tassie picked up Baxter and headed for the break room so she could grab his harness and leash.

"Baxter and I are going over there to talk to Tristan," she told her sister.

Abby nodded and waved, not glancing up from the computer.

Hug in a Mug lived up to its name in every sense of the word. The interior was all warm wood tones and cozy seating areas and the whole shop was filled with the delicious scent of coffee. Even though Tassie would pick a cup of hot tea over coffee any day, she loved the aroma of the latter. Luckily, Hug in a Mug sold both.

But unfortunately, she didn't have time to get her usual cinnamon chai tea because Tristan had picked up his order and was already heading for the door. Tall and lanky, he wore a slouch knit beanie over shaggy light brown hair and wire-rimmed glasses. He didn't look like a murderer.

He had his nose buried in his phone as he walked, so he didn't see Tassie quickly moving to intercept him until she was right in front of him.

"Tristan Meyers," she said. "Conrad Meyers' son, right?"

She thought she should probably check to make sure he was actually the right guy before interrogating him. That would be embarrassing.

"Yeah." Hazel eyes regarded her warily. "Are you a reporter?"

"A reporter?" she repeated, confused for a moment before realization dawned on her. "No! I'm a friend of Sara's." She probably should have led with that first. "Tassie Drake. I own Pupcakes—across the street."

Tristan glanced over her shoulder in the direction she pointed, then nodded. "Right. Sara mentioned you. Sorry I thought you were a reporter. It's just that people have been hounding me everywhere I go since my old man got murdered."

And now, he'd be able to add her to the list.

Tassie gestured toward a table. "Do you have a minute to talk?"

"Um…" He checked his phone to see what time it was. "Sure."

When they were seated, she settled Baxter on her lap. "I wanted to thank you for helping Sara find a lawyer."

He leaned forward, wrapping his hands around the to-go cup, a bewildered expression on his face. "I can't believe the cops think she killed my old man."

Tassie ran her hand over Baxter's ears. "Were you and your father close?"

"Close?" Tristan snorted. "No. I hated the guy." He flushed, as if realizing what he'd just said. "That must sound crappy considering he's dead and all. But he was never really a father to me before my parents were divorced and even less of one after they split up."

The bitterness in Tristan's voice hung in the air and she felt her heart go out to him.

"I'm sorry," she said, and genuinely meant it. Her parents might drive her crazy at times—whose didn't?—but she wouldn't trade them for anything. It sounded like Tristan hadn't been so fortunate. At least not when it came to Conrad. "It must have been difficult for you."

On the other side of the table, Tristan frowned down at his coffee cup with a shrug. "It is what it is. My old man could never accept me for who I am. He wanted a son who was into deep sea fishing as much as he was. Didn't matter to him that I got seasick every time I went out on the boat. Never mind that I couldn't catch a fish to save my life. He took me out on the water with him as soon as I could walk. He never got that his thing wasn't my thing. I wanted to be a musician not become a partner in his charter fishing business and eventually take it over. He hated my music. Said it was a waste of time."

"Sara told me that you and she stopped by your father's house a few weeks ago," Tassie said.

"Yeah." Tristan picked up his cup and took a drink. "It was pretty much a disaster."

"That's what she said. Do you have any idea what he wanted to talk to you about?"

His mouth twisted wryly. "He came to the club that night, so I know *exactly* what he wanted to talk to me about. He thought he could buy his way back into my life with all that money he won in the lottery."

She frowned. "I don't understand."

"He offered to give me half of the money that he won," Tristan said. "The only catch was that I had to hang out with him."

Whoa. Half of the millions Conrad won was...well...still millions.

"That's a lot of cash," Tassie said. "What did you tell him?"

"I told him what he could do with his money."

Huh. Well that kind of poked a big fat hole in her theory that Tristan might have killed his father for the money. Unless he wanted *all* the money without the strings attached. If Conrad left Tristan the money, that is.

Tristan let out a disgusted snort. "Even dead, my old man is still messing up my life."

"What do you mean?"

"He gets himself murdered right after Sara gets into a fight with him and now the woman I care about could go to prison." He shook his head. "I should have gone with her to the dog park that day. If I had, none of this would have happened."

Tassie had been wondering how to work Tristan's alibi into the conversation. Even though Sara had told her that Tristan said he was home alone working on a song, she wanted to check to make sure he didn't change his story.

"Where were you?" she asked.

"Home," he said. "I was writing a new song."

"With the guys in your band?"

She secretly hoped he'd forgotten he was hanging out with his band so he'd have an alibi because she honestly didn't want Sara's boyfriend to turn out to be the murderer. He seemed like a nice guy and he obviously cared for her.

But Tristan shook his head. "Nah. I don't like any distractions when I'm writing."

Drats.

He took out his phone to check the time. "I gotta go meet up with the band. It was nice meeting you."

"You too," she said. "Tell Sara I said hello."

Tassie looked at Baxter, letting out a sigh. "Well, Tristan didn't do anything to make me think he murdered his father, but he doesn't have an alibi, so I'm still going to consider him a suspect. What do you think?"

In answer, Baxter booped her nose with his.

When Tassie walked into Pupcakes with Baxter a few minutes later, Abby was talking to a guy at the counter. Tassie didn't recognize him, but then again, she didn't know everyone on sight from looking at the back of their head. Whoever the man was, Baxter was already wagging his tail in greeting.

"Tassie!" Abby said, beaming at her from the other side of the counter even as the guy turned around. "This is Isaac Bridger, the dog psychologist Finn and I have been seeing. Isaac, this is my sister, Tassie, and her dog, Baxter."

Tassie smiled. "Nice meeting you. Abby's told me so much about you."

It wasn't a lie. Abby had been talking nearly constantly about Isaac ever since her first session with him. She'd already fallen for the guy with a thud.

He laughed. "Nice to meet you too."

"Isaac came in to pick up some treats for his dog," Abby explained.

He flashed her sister a grin. "And to change the location of our next session to the dog park."

"Yes!" Abby said a little breathlessly. "Finn and I will be there."

Isaac and her sister gazed at each other for so long that Tassie wondered if she and Baxter should give them some privacy, but finally, the dog psychologist picked up his bag of goodies, petted Baxter and Finn, and then headed for the door.

Smiling, Abby returned the wave he gave her as he left.

"You should tell him the truth," Tassie said the moment Isaac was out the door.

"I'm going to tell him the truth," her sister said at the same time.

Tassie looked at her in surprise. "Well, that was easy. I thought for sure you'd disagree with me."

Abby shrugged. "Somewhere in between him walking in that door after you went over to Hug in a Mug and him walking back out, I realized that if I want to have anything real with him in the future, I have to be honest with him now."

Tassie stared at her sister, stunned. "I'm proud of you."

Abby grinned. "I have my moments. So, how was your conversation with Tristan?"

Tassie quickly filled her in on what Conrad's son had told her, adding that she wasn't ready to definitively say whether Tristan was the killer or not.

"He didn't suspect you were investigating his father's murder, did he?" Abby asked, concern in her voice.

"I don't think so." Tassie frowned. "Why?"

"Because after you talked to Belinda at the gallery last night she kept stealing glances at you like she was afraid you knew something." Her sister sighed. "Just be careful, okay."

"I will," Tassie promised.

Abby nodded, but still looked worried.

Tassie was concerned too, but for a different reason. The longer it took her to find Conrad's murderer, the more likely that person was going to get away with it and Sara was going to take the fall.

Chapter 14

Unfortunately, Tassie couldn't talk to Conrad's business partner, David Campbell, until the following morning because he was out with a group on a charter that afternoon and wouldn't be back until sunset. Talking to a suspect in a murder at that person's place of work after hours with no one around wasn't the smart thing to do so she spent the rest of the day baking cookies, talking to customers, and playing with Baxter.

That night, she did some investigating online. Conrad's social media didn't give her any clues as to who murdered him. Not that she expected it to. There were lots of photos of the ocean and fishing boats as well as him displaying various fish he'd caught. It was kind of weird to reconcile the mean man who gave everyone who got near his lawn a dirty look with the one smiling for the camera.

She was about to close his Facebook page when she realized he'd tagged Oliver Bolton—the man she'd found buried in Conrad's backyard—in quite a few photos.

Curious, she clicked on Oliver's name. It wouldn't help her figure out who murdered Conrad, but it might give some insight as to why he killed Oliver, a man who was supposed to be his friend.

Alas, Oliver's Facebook page didn't tell her much of anything either. Like Conrad, he'd posted a ton of memes related to fishing as well as pictures of him on various fishing excursions. The fish he'd caught were bigger than the fish Conrad had, but she didn't think that was a motive to murder someone.

There was also a photo Oliver had posted of him as a toddler with his parents on their anniversary. The picture was taken before cell phone cameras so not only wasn't it the highest resolution, but Oliver had obviously scanned and uploaded it. Even so, they looked like they'd been happy.

Since she was already on Facebook anyway, Tassie impulsively checked to see if Jack was on there too. More importantly, if he was, hopefully, he hadn't set his page to private.

He was on there.

And it wasn't set to private.

Bingo!

Jack didn't post a ton, but the photos he'd uploaded made Tassie smile. From how many of them were taken outdoors, he clearly loved communing with nature. He didn't spend all his time skiing and hiking though. There were lots of pictures indoors too. Some were with family, others with friends, but it was the pics of him with Gus that she loved the most. She couldn't have picked a favorite if she had to, although the ones of him with his dog right after he rescued the Lab mix were absolutely precious.

So, even though Tassie hadn't found anything to help her solve Conrad's murder, she had fun getting to know a little more about Jack. She almost sent him a friend request but chickened out at the last minute. Maybe she would after they had a few more "dates" at the dog park.

Or they solved Conrad's murder, whichever came first.

If she were lucky, maybe that'd be today.

For Reel Sportfishing was located about a mile past the dog park so Tassie decided to drive instead of walk. Like many places in Bluewater Bay, they'd renovated an older home and turned it into a business. White siding with navy-blue shutters, it had a cute front porch with a few rocking chairs as well as a walkway with a railing that led down to the water's edge and the fishing boats docked there.

After parking her SUV, Tassie made her way to the front door, Baxter in her arms. She wasn't sure what kind of stuff could be lying around on the ground outside a charter fishing business, and she didn't want to take any chances with his little feet.

"Okay, Baxter," she said. "Put on your game face."

The bell above the door rang as Tassie opened it and walked inside. Photos of smiling fishermen and women proudly displaying their catches, artistic pictures of fishing boats, and colorful shots of the bay and ocean at sunrise and sunset decorated the walls to either side of the room. She even spotted Conrad in some of the photos.

"May I help you?"

Tassie dragged her attention away from the pictures to find the woman behind the counter regarding her with a friendly smile. Mid-forties, she had shoulder-length curly black hair and wore a tee with the words *For Reel Sportfishing* and the company's logo on it.

"I'm looking for David Campbell," Tassie said.

"He's out back by the dock. We've got an afternoon charter leaving in an hour or so."

Thanking her, Tassie quickly made her way out of the building and down the sloping walkway to the dock behind the building. Having lived in Bluewater Bay her whole life, she was no stranger to boats. Oddly enough though, she'd never been on one specifically for fishing. Probably because she didn't eat seafood.

There were two boats docked behind For Reel named Reel Deal Two and Reel Deal Three. Since Reel Deal One was nowhere in sight, she assumed that meant it was out with a charter. About fifteen or so people were hanging around the area, filling out paperwork and checking gear. Baxter seemed as interested in everything going on as she was.

Tassie glanced around, trying to find David. She'd seen his photo on For Reel Sportfishing's website, but couldn't find him among the group.

"Looking for someone?"

She turned to see a tall man regarding her curiously—emphasis on tall. In his early thirties, he wore a heavy sweater under a waterproof jacket as well as a knit cap. He was kind of cute in a lumberjack way. Or rather, a deep-sea fisherman way, she supposed.

"David Campbell," she said. "The woman I talked to inside said he'd be down here."

"Sure is," the man said. "Come on. He's right over here."

Tassie followed him through the crowd of people to the far end of the dock.

"David," he said when they reached the boat named For Reel Two and the stocky dark-haired man moving around on it. "Someone to see you."

"Thanks, Allen." Wiping his hands on the rag he held, David stepped off the boat and walked over to them as the other man—Allen—moved over to the craft. "What can I help you with?"

"I was hoping I could ask you a few questions about Conrad," she said.

His eyes narrowed. "You a reporter?"

Why did everyone ask her that?

"No. I'm a..."

Drats. She couldn't very well say she was a friend of the woman accused of murdering Conrad. If David was the real killer, that'd only put his guard up.

"True crime podcaster," she finally said, mostly because it was the first thing that came to mind.

He grunted at that, though she couldn't tell if it was because he liked podcasts or hated them. "You doing an episode on Conrad's murder?"

Tassie nodded. "Do you have a few minutes to talk?"

"Sure." Towel still in hand, he folded his arms. "What do you want to know?"

Whether you murdered him or not.

Nope. She couldn't say that.

"Did Conrad have any enemies?"

David let out a harsh laugh. "Depends on how you define enemies. It might be easier to ask if he had any friends."

"Which were you?" she asked.

"Depended on the day," he said.

That was a surprisingly honest answer considering Conrad had been murdered.

"Were you more friends or enemies lately?"

His mouth tightened. "We were good once. I'd like to say we were the same friends we were when we first started the business twenty years ago, but we weren't. Haven't been for a long time."

Over by the boat, Allen glanced their way but didn't say anything.

"What happened?" she asked.

"He won the lottery, for one thing," David grumbled. "We'd talked about buying more boats and hiring additional captains for years, so I figured when he came into all that money, he'd put some of it into the business. Instead, the jerk told me that he was dissolving our partnership and opening his own charter fishing company. Not only that, but he was going to take our best customers with him. There was no way I was going to let that happen. And I told him that too."

Tassie held her breath. Could this be the confession she'd been waiting for? Having your business partner betray you and threaten to open his own company and steal your best customers sounded like a motive for murder if she'd ever heard one.

"When you say you weren't going to let that happen, you mean...?" she prompted.

"I was going to hire a lawyer," he said. "I wasn't sure if I could keep Conrad from dissolving the partnership, but I was sure going to try."

Tassie didn't have a law degree so she wasn't sure about that either. She should have known that David wouldn't confess to murder just like that. It would have been too easy.

"But then Conrad was murdered," she said.

She left out the word *conveniently*.

David let out a snort. "Whoever did it saved me some money on legal fees, I can tell you that."

"I'm sure." She glanced over at the group of people waiting for their excursion to go out then turned back to David. "I heard that Oliver Bolton, the man found buried in Conrad's backyard, was a regular on your charters."

David's brow furrowed, what seemed like genuine sadness filling his eyes. "Yeah, he was. Shame what happened to him. Oliver was a good man." He glanced at Allen. "Isn't that right?"

"Sure was," Allen said, walking over to join them. "Came fishing with us once a week like clockwork. We were all stunned when we heard he'd been murdered."

"*And* buried in Conrad's backyard," David added.

Tassie looked from one man to the other. "Do you think Conrad killed Oliver?"

David frowned again. "Considering he was buried in Conrad's yard, who else could have done it?"

"It's the only thing that makes sense," Allen agreed. "Kinda weird. Conrad and Oliver were pretty tight. They must have had some kind of falling out I guess."

"When did you see Oliver last?" she asked.

David thought a moment. "Had to be a few weeks ago."

"Yeah," Allen said. "I was wondering where he was when I didn't see his name on any of the charters going out. He went fishing once a week like clockwork."

Laughter from the people further down the dock drifted in their direction and David glanced that way.

"I've gotta get this charter out," he said to Tassie. "Hope you got enough for your podcast. Make sure you let the world know what a lowlife Conrad was, huh? I don't want anyone feeling sorry that creep is dead."

Tassie watched him make his way over to the waiting fishermen. Well, those were certainly strong words.

"Wow. He really didn't like Conrad, did he?" she said. "Then again, Conrad *was* going to steal his business so there's that."

"I'm not sure it was just his business that David was worried about Conrad stealing."

Tassie turned to look at Allen. "What do you mean?"

He hesitated, a dilemma clearly going on in his head. "I shouldn't say anything."

Grrr. Tassie grit her teeth. Then he shouldn't have brought it up in the first place. If he knew something that tied David to Conrad's murder, she needed to find out what it was.

"Come on. You can't leave me hanging like that," she said. "I promise it won't end up on the podcast."

That *was* true.

Allen thought a moment before letting out a sigh. "Okay. But you didn't hear it from me." His gaze went to his boss then back to her. "Rumor is that David's wife was cheating on him. Not sure with who, but the other guys and I think she was having an affair with Conrad."

Tassie gaped, not sure what to say to that bombshell.

David's wife was cheating on him with *Conrad*? Maybe it was all that lottery money he won?

"Was David here at work around the time Conrad was murdered?" she asked.

"I don't know. I was off that day. Kim at the front desk would probably know." Allen gazed at her for a moment. "I gotta go, but if you need anything else for your podcast, you can come back, if you want. I'd be glad to talk to you some more."

Was he blushing a little? She gave him a smile. "Thanks. I will."

He nodded. "Take care."

Tassie stood there long after Allen walked away, trying to wrap her head around what the man had just told her. She couldn't imagine any woman having an affair with Conrad, no matter how hard she tried. But if David's wife *had* been having an affair with Conrad, then that gave him even more motive for murder.

Chapter 15

"I don't suppose we can simply go ask David's wife if she was having an affair with Conrad, huh?"

From the safe confines of his car seat in the SUV still parked outside For Reel Sportfishing, Baxter gave Tassie a pointed look.

"Yeah, I didn't think so." She sighed. "Well, if we can't talk to Mrs. Campbell, then we'll do the next best thing—talk to Estelle. If anyone knows who's cheating with whom, it's Bluewater Bay's foremost gossip."

There was only one problem. Today was Snicker's birthday and Estelle had mentioned on her Facebook page that she and Snickers would be spending the day with her sister and her dog in Cutler's Cove. She'd have to wait until tomorrow to talk to Estelle.

As for asking Kim at the front desk whether David was at work when Conrad was murdered that was a no-go too. Kim would have wondered why Tassie hadn't simply asked David when she'd talked to him. And if Kim mentioned it to David, it might make him suspicious. She'd have to come up with another way to find out.

Which was probably a good thing since she had to get back to Pupcakes and mind the shop so Abby could meet up with Isaac at the dog park.

Fifteen minutes later, Tassie walked into the doggy bakery to find several customers and their dogs shopping for treats. Waving at them, she hurried over to where Abby was behind the counter eagerly waiting for her.

Her sister grabbed her purse from one of the drawers behind the counter along with Finn's harness and leash. "Okay, we're off to the dog park to see Isaac. Wish me luck."

Tassie laughed. "You got this."

By the time the last customer had picked out their treats and left, Tassie had come up with a plan to find out if David had an alibi for the time of Conrad's murder. Thanks to Lucy talking her into trying out with her for the spring play in high school, she had to learn how to do a southern accent. Even though she hadn't done it in years, she was confident she could still pull it off. She had to hope that the woman at the front desk didn't recognize her voice. Or remember that there wasn't a family from Mississippi up here on vacation. Now, she simply needed a few minutes to make a phone call between customers. If someone walked in while she was on the phone, she'd have a lot of explaining to do.

From where he relaxed on his plush bed, Baxter watched as she picked up her cell phone and opened Google.

"Show time," she told Baxter.

Quickly finding the number for David's charter fishing company, she dialed, then waited.

"For Reel Sportfishing. This is Kim," a woman's voice answered.

"Hey there, sugar. I sure hope you can help me," Tassie said, pitching her voice a little higher and drawing out the words a little longer. "My family and I are up here on vacation from Mississippi and did some charter fishing the other day. We had such a wonderful time that I wanted to send a gift basket to the captain of the boat as a thank you. Thing is, I can't remember his name for the life of me."

"That's not a problem," Kim said. "What day did you and your family take the charter?"

"Monday."

"Morning, afternoon, or full day?"

Oh, drats.

"Afternoon," Tassie said hesitantly. "Then again, we had so much fun that it could have been the full day. You know how time flies!"

On the other end of the line, she heard Kim tapping on the computer. "If you went on the afternoon charter, Bill was the captain. And for the full day, Gary."

"Bill or Gary. I thought it was Darren or Derrick. I really am so bad with names, but I thought it started with a D."

"The only charter captain we have whose name starts with a D is David and he left early that day, so Bill covered the afternoon charter."

"He did?" Tassie asked. "Are you sure?"

"I'm sure," Kim said.

"That was very helpful," Tassie said. "Thank you so much."

She hung up and looked at Baxter excitedly. "Did you hear that? David didn't have an alibi for the time of the murder. Unless he was at the dentist or something, of course. But for our purposes, we're going to say he wasn't. Which makes him our number one suspect!"

Of course, she still had to confirm his wife had been having an affair with Conrad. And make sure he didn't have an alibi she wasn't aware of.

But one thing at a time.

Also, hopefully, Kim didn't tell Bill or Gary about the gift basket because neither of them was getting one.

Abby came back a little while later, a beaming smile on her face. Beside her, Finn seemed equally happy.

Tassie grinned. "I take it that things went well with Isaac."

"They did!" Abby exclaimed. "I admitted that I only booked a session for Finn so that I could meet him, and he told me that he'd already figured that out. We're having dinner tonight and I can't wait!" She bent to get Finn out of his harness, then gave him a pat. "Oh! I just realized! I ran out so fast before that I didn't get to ask what happened at the charter fishing place."

While they straightened up the shelves and figured out what treats they needed to bake more of, Tassie filled her in on everything she'd learned at For Reel Sportfishing.

"After we close, I'm going to stop by the police station and talk to Jack," she added.

Abby waved her hand. "Why don't you go now? I'll lock up."

"You sure?"

Her sister nodded. "Yeah. Go."

Five minutes later, Tassie and Baxter were heading for the door.

"Have fun with Isaac tonight," she told her sister.

The police station was only a few doors down from Pupcakes so it didn't take long for her and Baxter to get there. Emily Miller, the uniformed officer at the counter, was on the phone when they walked in. She gave Tassie a wave as she and Baxter swung open the half door that divided the lobby from the main part of the station. Since Tassie stopped by to see Lucy regularly, all the cops knew her.

Lucy was at her desk, headset on, fingers tapping away at her keyboard. When she caught sight of Tassie and Baxter, she held up a finger, said something into her mic to the patrol officer she was talking to, then smiled and waved them over.

"I'm glad you're here," Lucy said. "I've checked out half of the restaurants on the list you gave me and think I have a winner, but I'm going to see what the rest of the places offer in regard to catering just to make sure."

"Excellent," Tassie said. "I owe you big."

"Don't think I won't remember you said that when Andrew and I want a night out and need a babysitter."

"Deal," Tassie said with a laugh.

She looked around what Lucy always referred to as the bullpen. In addition to Lucy's desk, there were four other desks the uniformed officers used when they were on duty, all of which were empty at the moment. There were two offices off the main room as well, one belonging to the chief of police, Hugh Pennington, and the other to Jack, but both doors were closed.

"Is Jack here?" she asked.

Before Lucy could answer, the door to his office opened and he strode out. Jack stopped when he saw her, clearly surprised.

"Hey," he said, flashing her a grin.

"Hey. I was just looking for you," she said, returning his smile as he walked over to her. "I have some stuff that could help with the investigation into Conrad's murder. Do you have a minute?"

"I was just heading out to grab something to eat," he said. "We can talk over dinner."

"Um, I..." Tassie stammered.

Now, it was her turn to be surprised.

Beside Tassie, Baxter wagged his tail happily, while behind Jack, from where she was still seated at her desk, Lucy nodded, her head nodding up and down like one of those bobblehead dolls.

"My treat," he said. "You can even pick the restaurant."

Tassie considered that. "Okay. We can go to The General Store. The food is always delicious there, but more importantly, it's dog friendly."

"Sounds good to me," Jack said.

Over at her desk, Lucy gave Tassie a big smile and a thumbs-up.

She truly was incorrigible.

Chapter 16

The dog-friendly dining room at The General Store was a heated outdoor seating area with plenty of colorful tables. While a little too cold in the fall and winter to sit out there, spring and summer were perfect for it. Tassie and Jack weren't the only ones taking advantage of the weather and she waved to the other people and dogs she knew as they followed the hostess to their table.

"Everyone says the lobster rolls here are out of this world," Tassie said as they both read over the menu. She didn't know why she bothered looking at it. She could recite everything on it by heart.

Across the table from her, Jack made a face. "So I heard, but I'm not a big seafood lover."

Tassie did a double take. "Seriously?"

He gave her what could almost be called a sheepish look. "I know. I know. I should have considered that Bluewater Bay is famous for its seafood before I moved here."

She laughed. "That's not it. I was going to say that I don't like seafood either."

"Wait a minute. Didn't you grow up here?"

"Yup. My mom and dad moved here after veterinary school to take over old Doc Webster's practice."

He thought a moment. "Your parents are The Doctors Drake Animal Clinic?"

Tassie sipped her iced tea. "That's them."

"Considering I'm a detective, I should have put that together," he said. "Any other brothers and sisters?"

She paused before setting her glass on the table. "An older brother."

Her voice broke a little like it always did whenever she talked about Nolan. After all these years, it shouldn't, and yet, she couldn't seem to control it.

Across from her, Jack frowned. "I'm sorry. I didn't realize he was..."

Dead.

He left the word unsaid.

She shook her head. "He isn't. At least...I don't think he is. I hope not."

Now, Jack look confused.

"Nolan is ten years older than me," she explained. "He left Bluewater Bay when he was eighteen."

"And he didn't stay in contact with your family?" Jack asked. "Was there some kind of falling out between him and your parents?"

She gave him a half-hearted shrug. "Abby and I were in school the day Nolan left but apparently he had some kind of huge argument with my mom and dad right before he left. My parents won't ever talk about it, so whatever the fight was about, it must have been really bad."

Jack's brow furrowed. "That's rough. Were you close to your brother before he left?"

She couldn't help but smile. "Yeah. When Abby and I were little, he'd read us bedtime stories and come to our tea parties. I hate that we might never know why he left."

Jack looked like he would have said more but the server's arrival interrupted him. They both decided on the chicken Marsala and a side salad. And for Baxter, a small bowl of plain baked chicken.

"Since you love animals, I'm surprised you didn't follow in your parents' footsteps and become a vet," Jack said after the man left, clearly wanting to talk about something that didn't make her so melancholy.

She was completely fine with that.

"When I was a kid, that's what I wanted to be, but after I passed out when we dissected frogs in middle school, I realized that being a vet wasn't in the cards." She smiled and reached down to caress Baxter's head where he sat beside her chair. "I'm glad because instead, I get to bake doggy treats and go to work with my best friend every day."

And she wouldn't trade it for anything.

"How about you?" she asked as they started on their salads.

He glanced at her as he picked up his fork, eyes twinkling. "Did I want to become a vet?"

"No." She laughed. "I meant, did you always want to be a cop?"

Jack chuckled. "Yeah, I know. I'm just messing with you." He speared a tomato with his fork and shook his head. "Nah. I wasn't sure what I wanted to do with my life until a buddy's father came in for career day in high school. He made his job as a cop sound so cool to sixteen-year-old me that I couldn't graduate fast enough so I could apply to the academy."

She could see that. "Did your buddy become a cop too?"

"Actually, he ended up getting arrested and is in prison for felony theft."

"Wow. I guess that apple fell far from the tree," she said as their dinner arrived. "So, is being a cop as cool as you thought it would be."

Jack waited to answer until their server had placed their dinner on the table and the small bowl of chicken on the floor in front of Baxter.

"Most days," he said.

"And the other days?"

"I'm usually stuck doing mountains of paperwork."

"Thankfully, my sister does most of that side of the business," she said. "What do your parents think of you being a cop?"

He picked up his knife and fork with a shrug. "My parents and sister mostly worry. They were relieved when I took a job in a small town like Bluewater Bay. Well, until they heard there'd been a murder on my first day."

She groaned. "I can imagine."

"Yeah, I definitely didn't have murder on my bingo card, that's for sure."

"But I can see why you like doing what you do," she said. "This investigation stuff is kind of fun."

He glanced up from cutting his chicken, mouth twitching. "Should I be concerned you'll be coming for my job soon?"

Tassie let out an amused snort. "Not even close. I'll stick to amateur detective status, thank you very much. Speaking of which, I think I might know who murdered Conrad."

"Okay," he said. "Let's hear it."

She took a deep breath. "Actually, I have a few possibilities, so I'll tell you what I learned about each of them, starting with Conrad's ex-wife, Belinda."

"She has an alibi for the time of the murder."

"If she hired someone to kill Conrad, then it doesn't matter if she has an alibi."

Jack paused, fork halfway to his mouth. That definitely got his attention.

"Belinda hosted a bring-your-dog-to-the-gallery event the other night so, of course, Baxter and I went because I wanted to talk to her about Conrad," Tassie explained, reaching for her iced tea. "I overheard her talking on the phone telling someone she'd Venmo them for something they did for her that she didn't want anyone to find out about."

He ate the piece of chicken still poised on his fork, chewing slowly as he considered that. "And you think she was talking to a hitman."

"Don't you?"

"I agree that it's suspicious but that doesn't necessarily mean she was on the phone with a hitman," he said. "I'll try to get a warrant for her phone records. See if we can find out who she was talking to."

"Good. Because she definitely didn't like her ex. I think the fact that he didn't play the lottery before they got divorced makes her hate him even more. The way she sees it, she could have gotten more alimony. She said as much."

Tassie glanced at Baxter to see if he'd finished his dinner. He had and was currently licking the bowl clean.

"Belinda's hoping Conrad left his fortune to their son, Tristan," she added, turning her attention back to Jack. "Which brings me to my next suspect. Though I don't think he's much of one since he doesn't seem to want anything to do with his father or his father's money."

"That doesn't mean he didn't have a different motive," Jack pointed out.

She smothered a piece of chicken in wine sauce, then popped it into her mouth. Mmm. It was the perfect combination of flavors. "I thought of that. He certainly despised his father. Can you believe Conrad tried to bribe Tristan into spending time with him for half of the lottery money he won? What kind of person does that?"

"Usually the type who would do anything to get his hands on that kind of money himself," Jack said.

"You have a point there," she agreed. "But while Tristan was angry at Conrad for a lot of things, in addition to offering him all that money, I don't think he murdered his father."

Jack frowned. "Yeah, I didn't get that vibe when I talked to him either."

"Now, Conrad's business partner, on the other hand, is a different story," Tassie said. "He's livid that Conrad didn't put some of the money he won into their fishing charter business and instead, intended to dissolve their partnership. Oh, *and* rumor has it that his wife was cheating on him with Conrad. Plus, I'm pretty sure David doesn't have an alibi for the time of Conrad's murder."

"He doesn't. I checked," Jack said. "I didn't know the part about his wife having an affair though. That's interesting."

"And a motive for murder. Only I'm not sure she was having an affair," Tassie clarified. "But I know someone who will."

"Who?"

She gave him a smile. "An amateur detective never reveals her sources."

"I'm pretty sure that's a reporter."

Tassie shrugged. "Tomayto-tomahto."

His mouth curved. "You'd make a good one, by the way."

"I'm going to take that as a compliment."

Jack chuckled softly. "Good. Because I meant it as one."

They ate in silence for a few moments before Jack spoke.

"I don't think Sara did it, you know," he said quietly. "But apparently, there's a baking competition in Bluewater Bay in a few weeks with a camera crew from a TV show and everything, and the mayor doesn't—and by extension, the chief of police—want a murder hovering over the event like a dark cloud, so they want this case closed quickly. Unfortunately, there's no other evidence to suggest that someone other than Sara killed him. There was no sign of forced entry into the house, and the only readable fingerprints on the murder weapon belonged to Sara."

"What about the shoe print?"

"Couldn't tell much from the partial. It could belong to anyone."

Tassie frowned. "Could someone have already been hiding in Conrad's house while Sara fought with him?"

"It's possible," he agreed. "The problem is that no one saw anyone entering or leaving Conrad's home."

"This would be a lot easier if the man had security cameras," she muttered.

Jack snorted. "Tell me about it. But unless we figure out who really killed Conrad, there's a good chance that Sara could be going to jail not only for his murder but also for Oliver's."

Tassie couldn't help but notice that he'd used the word *we*, and she'd be lying if she said she didn't like it. Hopefully, he was including her in that and not simply referring to his fellow police officers.

The other part of what he said was disturbing though. "Oliver's murder? She didn't even know him."

At least Tassie didn't think she did.

"I know," Jack said. "But the mayor has some convoluted theory about Sara killing Oliver and burying him in Conrad's backyard to frame him and when that didn't work, she murdered Conrad."

"Wow. That *is* convoluted."

"Regardless, your friend could be looking at a double-murder charge."

"Then we need to figure out who did it," she said firmly. "And soon."

Jack regarded her thoughtfully. "You know, when you first wanted to get involved in this whole thing, I didn't want you anywhere near the case, but I have to admit I'm impressed by your investigative skills."

She smiled. "I told you I watch a lot of murder mysteries."

His mouth curved. "As long as you don't do anything dangerous, I'm okay with you doing it."

"Understood."

Hey, she didn't want to do anything dangerous either.

They spent the rest of dinner and a good portion of dessert—a decadent slice of chocolate cake that they shared—continuing to talk about both murder investigations. Jack agreed with her that Conrad had almost certainly killed Oliver, even if the people at For Reel Sportfishing were surprised considering the two men had appeared to be friends. Tassie couldn't imagine anyone being chummy with Conrad, but at least one murder seemed to be solved. Now, they had to find enough evidence to convince the mayor and chief of police.

"Thank you for dinner," Tassie said as Jack walked her and Baxter back to where her SUV was parked near Pupcakes.

Now that it was dark, it was cooler than it'd been before, and she carried Baxter in her arms to keep him warmer. Luckily, he liked when she held him. Maybe because it let him see more from this vantage point.

She walked a little closer to Jack. Not because she was cold but because she liked being near him.

"You're very welcome," Jack said. "Maybe we can do it again."

She grinned. "I'd like that. And next time, you can bring Gus."

"He'd definitely like that." He glanced at her shop. She and Abby left the lights on inside even at night so everything was clearly visible, including the cute Easter display she and Baxter had put together the other day. Well, mostly her, she supposed. But her Chiweenie had helped. "I still have to stop by Pupcakes with him."

"Definitely!" Tassie slowed to a stop when they got to her SUV, turning toward him. "Well, this is me."

Jack stopped too. "I'll let you know if I get anything from Belinda's phone records."

"And I'll let you know if I find out whether David's wife was cheating on him with Conrad or not."

As they stood there gazing at each other, Tassie got the feeling Jack wanted to kiss her. Which was perfectly a-okay with her. She wanted to kiss him too.

She didn't know who leaned closer to the other first, but his lips were just inches away from hers when

Baxter let out a sharp bark, interrupting whatever smooching was going to happen. She stepped back with an embarrassed laugh even as he did the same.

Since Baxter clearly liked Jack, she wasn't sure why he'd mind if the two of them kissed. She glanced at her fur baby to see what was up with him only to realize that he wasn't paying attention to them at all. Instead, he was focused on something down the street, ears and eyes on high alert.

While she was glad he hadn't suddenly changed his mind about liking Jack, unfortunately, the romantic moment that'd been there a moment ago now seemed to have disappeared.

Drats.

"Well, I guess Baxter sees something or someone he doesn't like over there," Jack chuckled.

"Yeah." She gave Baxter a kiss on the nose, then smiled. "I better get home."

"Drive safe." Jack petted her pooch on the head. "Goodnight, Baxter."

Tassie got Baxter all situated in the SUV, then gave Jack a wave as she turned onto the street. He returned the gesture, watching her drive down the road before turning to continue along the sidewalk toward the police station. She knew because she snuck a peek at the rearview mirror to check.

She smiled, unable to help it. He was fun to be around.

"Did you have a good time tonight, Baxter?" she asked, glancing over her shoulder at him.

To her surprise, he was as alert as he'd been outside Pupcakes, his cute face filled with doggy concern as he looked out the window.

"What has you so uptight, baby?"

Whatever it was, he was still agitated by the time she pulled into her assigned parking space outside the townhouse they shared with Abby and Finn. Theirs was on the end of the row and painted a pretty colonial blue with white shutters. Two floors with a finished basement, it was perfect for the four of them. Tassie only wished it had a garage. Digging their vehicles out of the snow in the winter was brutal.

Shrugging into her crossbody bag, Tassie picked Baxter up, deciding to carry him instead of using the leash. Cuddling him close, she slowly turned in a half circle, showing him their surroundings.

"See?" she said. "Nothing's out there."

Baxter didn't seem convinced.

She looked around, her gaze fixed on the darkness beyond the parking lot but didn't see anything. That didn't mean there wasn't something there. What if Belinda had gotten the same hitman she'd hired to murder Conrad to come after her? Or what if David had figured out she thought he might be the killer and followed her when she'd left For Reel Sportfishing earlier that day so he could silence her?

Tassie suppressed a shiver. That was her overactive imagination talking again. There was no way they could know she suspected them. She'd been very careful when it came to that.

But Baxter had good instincts. If he thought something—or someone—was out there, then she was going to trust him.

Which meant they should get inside.

Tassie turned to head up the steps to the front door just as Abby pulled in, parking in the space beside hers.

"I'm surprised to see you home so early," Tassie said as her sister joined her even as she glanced at the trees again. Not that she could see anything anyway. "Did the date with Isaac go okay?"

Beside Abby, Finn wagged his tail happily. Thankfully, it seemed like neither of them sensed her anxiety or Baxter's.

"It went great!" Abby said. "Isaac has an early therapy session tomorrow morning, so we called it a night. We're getting together tomorrow."

"Yay! I want to hear all about it. And don't leave anything out!" Tassie waved her hand in a hurry-up motion. "Come on. Let's go inside."

"What about your date with Jack?" Abby asked. "Lucy texted to tell me that you and Baxter were having dinner with him."

Tassie laughed and unlocked the door. "It wasn't a date. We were talking about the murder investigation."

In her arms, Baxter gave her the side-eye, which she pointedly ignored.

Her sister regarded her skeptically. "Uh-huh."

"Okay," she said, glancing over her shoulder as she led the way into the entryway and flipped on the light. "I guess it was a date—kinda."

They almost kissed so that meant it was a date, right?

"I knew it!" Abby exclaimed, following at her heels. "Well, I want to hear all about it. And don't leave anything out!"

Tassie laughed as her sister playfully used her own words against her, relieved when Abby locked the deadbolt with the key. She might have an imagination that worked overtime, but that didn't mean there wasn't someone out there.

Chapter 17

"I'm going to run over to Gwen's to pick up some cupcakes for Estelle," Tassie said to her sister. "I figure that if I'm going to ply her for information, I should at least give her something in return."

Since she couldn't very well ask David's wife if she'd been having an affair with Conrad, Tassie would have to do the next best thing—talk to Estelle. The woman knew everything about everyone in town. Which was kind of a scary thing when she thought about it.

Tassie picked Baxter up and gave him a quick kiss on the head. "I'll be back in a few minutes and then we'll go see Estelle. Sound good?"

Baxter licked the tip of her nose in answer. Whereas he'd been wary of whatever was in the shadows last night, thankfully, he was back to his usual self this morning.

She looked at Abby. "You sure you don't mind running the store while I do some investigating today?"

Abby waved her hand. "Not at all. Isaac is coming over in a little while so if I need help, I'll ask him."

Tassie smiled but didn't say anything. She and Abby had chilled on the couch with Baxter and Finn as well as mugs of hot cocoa and talked for hours last night about their respective evenings. It was obvious that Abby liked Isaac a lot, and Tassie admitted she felt the same about Jack, even though she wasn't close to defining their relationship yet.

Were they friends?

Fellow dog lovers?

A couple?

They'd only gone on one date—if it was a date—so it was probably too early for them to be that.

Maybe they were simply two people working together to solve a murder?

Despite that almost-kiss last night, she wasn't quite sure.

Gwen, the owner of The Cozy Cupcakery, was helping another customer when Tassie walked in, so she smiled and waved at the petite blonde woman as she made her way to the counter. The delicious scent of chocolate enveloped Tassie followed by other scrumptious flavors. Vanilla, cinnamon, caramel, coconut, and peanut butter all swirled together in a delectable combination, and she took a deep breath, savoring it.

A few people worked at the bakery with Gwen and today it was a wiry guy with dark hair and glasses. You couldn't go wrong with any of the cupcakes Gwen baked, but Tassie decided to keep it simple with a four-pack of minis—one dark chocolate, one snickerdoodle, one salted caramel, and one chocolate chip. Unable to resist, she also bought two dark chocolate minis for her and Abby.

Catching Gwen's eye, Tassie gave her another wave as she headed for the door. It opened just as she reached it and she found herself face-to-face with Allen, the guy she'd spoken to yesterday at For Reel Sportfishing. The one who'd kind of flirted with her. Although, maybe saying face-to-face wasn't quite accurate considering he was practically seven foot tall.

"Hey," he said, grinning. "You're the woman with the true-crime podcast. From yesterday."

She glanced over her shoulder before nodding. Everyone in the Cupcakery knew who she was and also that she didn't have a podcast. She didn't want them overhearing and blowing her cover.

Tassie slipped through the door he was still holding open, giving him a smile. "Yeah. Allen, right?"

Grin broadening, he closed the door, stepping aside so they weren't blocking the entrance. "Right. Is your podcast available to download yet?"

Her *nonexistent* podcast. Nope.

"Not yet," she said.

He looked disappointed at that. "What's the name of the podcast? I'd really like to listen to the other episodes you've done."

She considered making something up but didn't want him searching for some podcast that didn't exist and getting suspicious.

"Um…" She gave him a sheepish look. "This is actually my first episode, so I'm still workshopping the name."

"Oh. That's cool." He thought a moment. "Are you going to tell your listeners that you think David killed Conrad?"

She opened her mouth then closed it again, not sure how to answer that. Since she'd never listened to a true crime podcast, she didn't know if the podcasters ever accused anybody. Probably not. That seemed like it would get them into legal hot water.

"No," she finally said. "I feel it's better to tell listeners what I learn and let the audience decide for themselves."

Allen nodded. "That makes sense. You know, David was acting kind of squirrelly after you talked to him yesterday."

That was interesting. And suspicious. "Did he say anything about Conrad?"

Preferably something incriminating.

"Not anything specific," Allen said. "It's crazy to think David could have killed him. Before Conrad won the lottery, they were best friends. David has this cabin near Waverly Lake and the two of them used to go up there all the time to freshwater fish."

"Do you happen to know where this cabin is?"

"Off of Millview Road," Allen said. "It's pretty easy to find. David and Conrad went up there a few days before Conrad was murdered. I think David thought it might help patch things up between them, but instead, they got into a huge scuffle."

Huh. More proof that David was the killer maybe. Tassie wondered if there was anything at the cabin that could tie him to Conrad's murder.

Allen cleared his throat, shifting from one foot to the other. "Um, I was wondering if maybe you'd want to grab coffee sometime?"

Tassie blinked. She'd been in a dating drought for months and now she had two guys interested in her. Admittedly, Allen was cute and seemed nice, and before she'd met Jack, she probably would have been interested in him. She'd never been into dating more than one man at a time though. Not that there was anything wrong with it, but it simply wasn't her thing.

"I'm kind of seeing someone," she said, wanting to let him down as gently as she could.

"Oh." Allen flushed. "Yeah, of course. I should have realized." He glanced around like he was trying to look at anything other than her right then. Finally, after staring down at his boots for a moment, he met her gaze again. "I better get going."

She nodded and opened her mouth to tell him that it was nice seeing him again, but he'd already ducked into The Cozy Cupcakery.

Well, that was all kinds of awkward.

Sighing, Tassie walked next door to her own shop. Hopefully, she hadn't hurt his feelings too much.

Chapter 18

Tassie walked into the Bluewater Bay Historical Society fifteen minutes later along with Baxter, armed with mini cupcakes and peanut butter doggy treats. She couldn't very well bring something for Estelle and not bring anything for Snickers.

Nestled among fir trees, red oaks, and maples, the historical society was in a beautifully restored two-story house with white clapboard and colonial blue shutters. Each room housed artifacts and memorabilia from different eras of the town's history dating all the way back to the 1700s. From old photos to antique furniture to meticulously preserved clothing to original maps and shipbuilding tools, there was something intriguing in every part of the place. Tassie wasn't sure how they did it, but the building even had an old-fashioned smell to it.

And while it might seem like Estelle spent all her time minding other people's business, she took her job as curator of the historical society very seriously. Bottom line, she knew her stuff.

Estelle was in the room the historical society had converted into an office doing something on the computer and looked up as Tassie wandered in with Baxter, her lips curving into a smile.

"Tassie!" she exclaimed. "What a lovely surprise! And you brought cupcakes! At least, I hope those are for me."

Laughing, Tassie set the bakery box down on the desk along with the bag of treats for Snickers. The Corgi sauntered from where he'd been chilling on his plush bed to greet a happy Baxter.

"They are," Tassie said. "And those are for your fur baby."

Estelle opened the bag to offer a tiny treat to Snickers. Then, at a smile and nod of approval from Tassie, handed one to Baxter as well. Estelle lifted the lid on the bakery box next, her eyes lighting up at the sight of the mini cupcakes.

"These look absolutely delicious," she said. "Would you like one?"

"As tempting as they are, I already treated myself to one when I stopped by The Cozy Cupcakery to pick these up for you." Tassie grinned. "Those are all yours."

Estelle chose the snickerdoodle one and carefully unwrapped it then took a nibble before looking at her. "Not that I don't love cupcakes, but something tells me that you didn't come all the way over here just to bring me a box of Gwen's goodies."

On the walk over, Tassie had toyed with the idea of saying she'd stopped by the historical society to check out the quilt exhibit that Estelle had mentioned the other night at the art gallery, but she got the feeling that the woman would see right through that.

Best to go with the direct approach.

"I need the scoop on something, and no one knows more about what goes on in Bluewater Bay than you," Tassie said.

Estelle preened, seeming to consider that as she finished the other half of the cupcake. Then she carefully closed the box, perched on the edge of the desk, and gazed at Tassie.

"Flattery will get you everywhere, every time, all the time. Cupcakes don't hurt of course," she said with an amused wink. "What do you want to know?"

"Was David Campbell's wife cheating on him with Conrad?"

"With Conrad?" Estelle stared at her for a moment, then laughed. "Good heavens, no! Whatever gave you that idea?"

"I overheard some people talking about it," she said casually. She didn't want Estelle to know she'd been playing amateur detective and asking around. "What makes you so sure she wasn't?"

"Because she's cheating on him with her personal trainer." Estelle let out a snort. "Talk about a cliché. You'd think the woman could be a little more original."

That was one way to look at it, Tassie supposed.

Estelle reached around behind her to pick up her coffee mug from the desk and took a sip. "Not that David cares, mind you."

Tassie frowned. "Why is that?"

"Because he's having an affair too."

"With whom?"

Estelle sipped her coffee. "The mayor's wife."

Tassie's mouth fell open. "No way!"

Estelle nodded. "Oh, yes. They've been secretly seeing each other for years. Even before her husband became mayor."

Wow. Tassie wondered if the mayor would be so quick to dismiss other suspects in Conrad's murder if he knew one of them was the man that his wife was cheating on him with.

"Conrad was actually seeing a woman in Cutler's Cove," Estelle continued. "A kindergarten teacher, I think."

Tassie was stunned for the second time in as many minutes. All the kindergarten teachers she knew were sweet and soft spoken and not the kind of women she'd picture getting involved with a man like Conrad.

"Do you know her name?" Tassie asked.

Estelle thought a moment. "Annette Henderson, I believe."

Tassie nodded, committing the name to memory. She'd like to talk to the woman and see if she could tell her anything about Conrad. Of course, she had to figure out how to locate her. Tassie didn't go to Bristol very much and didn't know anyone there so that might be tricky.

"What do you know about her?" Tassie asked.

"Not much," Estelle admitted with a sigh. "When it comes to networking, my reach does extend as far as Cutler's Cove. Unfortunately, Annette Henderson is rather a mystery." She smiled. "Speaking of which, what about you and Bluewater Bay's handsome new detective?"

Tassie did a double take. "What about us?"

Estelle's eyes twinkled. "A little birdie told me that the two of you went on a date last night."

Exactly who was part of this aforementioned network Estelle had? And why was Tassie having dinner with Jack something they considered important enough to report to her?

"It wasn't a date," Tassie insisted.

From where he sat on the floor, Baxter gave her the look—the one that said he knew she was being less than honest.

Okay, maybe she was.

"You know," Estelle said. "There's an old saying that if you share dessert with a man you just had dinner with, then it was most definitely a date."

Tassie gave her a look. "I'm pretty sure that no one has ever said that."

Estelle merely shrugged and took another sip of coffee.

"How do you know everything about everyone in town anyway?" Tassie asked.

Estelle smiled. "A good curator never reveals her sources."

Tassie wanted to point out that was reporters not curators, but then remembered she'd used the same line on Jack at dinner last night.

"Fair enough," she said with a laugh. "Thanks for the info."

"Thanks for the cupcakes and doggy treats. And if you need the scoop on anyone else, you know where to find me.

Pulling out her phone, Tassie texted her sister to tell her that she was tracking down a lead. As she'd expected, Abby was totally cool with that.

She had the best sister ever.

Slipping her cell into her crossbody bag, she started down the sidewalk toward the police station with Baxter. After talking to Estelle, she realized the best way to find Annette Henderson was to ask Jack for help in that department. Police always had all those fancy resources. They knew where people lived and what kind of car they drove. Stuff like that.

Besides, she'd promised him that she wouldn't do anything dangerous. And since wandering around the woods looking for the cabin of a suspected murderer probably fell into that category, he might want to go with her and Baxter.

She didn't remember that it was Saturday and Jack might not be working until she got to the police station, but the door to his office was open and the light was on. She said a quick hello to Henry, who was working the counter, as well as Ellie Walker, the weekend dispatcher, then walked over to Jack's office. He was standing behind his desk, staring down at something on the computer, a scowl on his face.

Tassie knocked lightly on the door. "Everything okay?"

He sighed. "I couldn't get a warrant for Belinda Meyers' phone. Apparently, overhearing her talk about paying for someone to do something she didn't want anyone to know about right after her ex gets murdered isn't considered probable cause. So, there's that."

"That stinks," she said. "But on the bright side, I think I might have another lead."

Tassie quickly told him about the conversations she'd had with Allen and Estelle. Leaving out the part about the deep-sea fisherman asking her out and the historical society curator inquiring about their date, of course.

"So," she said with a grin. "You feel like going for a hike?"

Chapter 19

The mid-morning sun bathed the blue water of the bay, turning it into hundreds of dazzling diamonds as she and Jack drove toward Cutler's Cove. Even though she'd lived there her whole life, Tassie was still awed by how beautiful this part of Maine was.

Even though you could practically see the town of Cutler's Cove from Bluewater Bay, thanks to all the inlets and coves, no one had ever built a bridge to connect the two, so it was a thirty-minute scenic drive along the bay.

And the company wasn't half bad either.

Tassie smiled at that. Actually, the company was absolutely perfect.

As for Cutler's Cove, it was just as quaint and cozy as Bluewater Bay but in a more whimsical, almost quirky way. Tassie couldn't put her finger on what made it so different. Maybe it was the peaked arch over the main street welcoming you to town or the gigantic bell buoy tipped on its side in the park near the harbor.

"That's a cool looking church," Jack remarked, gesturing with his chin as they drove along the harbor road.

Tassie followed his gaze to see him looking up at a big, beautiful building with turrets, bell tower, and stained glass up on a hill overlooking the harbor. "It used to be a church from the 1700s until the turn of the twenty-first century but now it's a private home. People say it's haunted."

His mouth twitched as he glanced at her. "Haunted, huh?"

"That's what they say. I heard they really do the house up right for Halloween."

He seemed to consider that. "Maybe we should come back here and check it out. If your game, I mean."

She laughed. "You're on."

That earned her a chuckle. "It's a date then."

And this time, Tassie wasn't left wondering if he was talking about an actual date or not either. After that almost kiss outside Pupcakes last night, she was fairly certain she knew exactly what he meant.

She and Jack had debated whether to pay Annette Henderson a visit first or check out David's cabin. They finally decided to talk to Annette before going to Waverly Lake. Mostly because they had no idea where the cabin was and if they ended up having to hike into the woods to get there, they didn't want to show up at Annette's door looking like it.

Tassie looked over her shoulder to check on Baxter. They'd stopped by her SUV to pick up his car carrier so he'd be safe in Jack's vehicle. Now, he sat there happily, listening to them talk.

As they continued along the road that ran along the harbor, the subject of Lucy's baby shower came up and before she realized it, Tassie was confessing about being a little nervous with both Gwen and Irene bringing cupcakes to the party.

He glanced at her, mouth twitching in amusement. "You going to need police presence at this thing?"

She laughed. "If cupcakes start flying, we just might."

Before he could reply, the map app on his phone directed them to turn right at the next street, then proceed to their destination, which was also on the right. As they pulled into the driveway of a small New England–style cottage house, Tassie realized again that it would have taken her forever to find Annette without Jack's help.

She clipped Baxter's leash on his harness even though she decided to hold him. If Annette had been dating Conrad, she might not be an animal lover either. If that was the case, Tassie would stay outside with her pup while Jack talked to the woman.

At first glance, the house appeared simple and unremarkable, but then she saw the symmetrical benches built into the front porch and the trellis above and realized they gave it a charm she hadn't noticed. And the Easter egg wreath that decorated the door was too cute.

As Jack reached out to ring the doorbell, Tassie hoped the woman was home. Otherwise, they'd driven out here for nothing. But a few moments later, the door opened, revealing a woman of around fifty with dark, curly hair starting to turn gray and a friendly face.

"Can I help you?" she asked.

"Annette Henderson?" Jack asked.

She nodded, looking curiously from him to Tassie and back again. "Yes."

Jack held up his badge. "Detective Sterling with the Bluewater Bay PD. I was wondering if we could talk to you about Conrad Meyers."

If Annette wondered why Jack hadn't mentioned Tassie by name or that she had Baxter with her, the woman didn't remark on it. Smile faltering a little, she let out a sigh and opened the door wider. "Of course. Come in."

Jack gestured for Tassie to go first, then followed.

Stepping inside, Tassie took a moment to look around while Annette closed the door behind them. Off to the right was a staircase up to the second floor and beyond the small entryway where they stood was the living room. It was a mix-and-match of vintage furniture, distressed wood, and neutral color scheme that seemed befitting of the cottage.

"Please sit," Annette said. "Can I get either of you anything to drink?"

"I'm good, thanks," Jack said, taking a seat in one of the two mismatched stuffed chairs.

Tassie nodded as she sat down on the couch, Baxter on her lap. "Me too."

Annette joined her on the other side of the couch. "Have you found Conrad's killer yet?"

Jack shook his head. "Not yet. When was the last time you saw him?"

"A few weeks ago." She gave them an apologetic look. "We weren't dating anymore—and even when we were, we didn't get together all that often. But I'll help you find out who murdered him in any way that I can."

Jack exchanged looks with Tassie before turning back to Annette. "Can I ask why you stopped seeing each other?"

She sighed. "He won the lottery."

That darn lottery again. It had to be the reason Conrad was murdered. She saw Jack glance at her again. Was he wondering if Annette and Conrad broke up because she wanted some of his lottery winnings?

"I'm afraid I don't follow," Jack said.

"After he won the lottery, Conrad changed," Annette explained. "He became obsessed with the money and how it might change his life. Especially when it came to his relationship with his son. He thought that having all those millions would make up for all those years he wasn't much of a father, I suppose." The woman must have seen the surprise on Tassie's face because she gave her a small smile. "Conrad and I may not have dated very long, but he did talk a lot about how strained his relationship with Tristan was. He was very open about it. When I told him that I didn't think flashing all that money was the way to repair it, he didn't want to hear it. Things between us went downhill quickly from there."

There seemed to be genuine sadness in Annette's eyes when she spoke. Even though they hadn't been seeing each other anymore, it appeared that she cared for Conrad on some level. Which would make her the first and only person Tassie had ever met to feel that way about the man.

"It was funny really," Annette continued, her gaze a little distant. "Conrad always said he thought that people who played the lottery were stupid—me included. That we might as well just throw our money away. Then, the first time he plays, he wins." She looked at them. "It almost didn't seem fair."

It didn't help that Conrad was such a jerk to boot. But Tassie didn't say that.

"Do you have any idea who might have wanted to kill Conrad?" Tassie asked.

The woman shook her head. "I don't. He mentioned his business partner was angry that he wanted to leave and start his own company after he won the lottery, but that the guy was all talk and no action." She frowned. "Do you think he's the one who killed Conrad?"

"We're still trying to determine that," Jack said smoothly.

"Did Conrad ever mention a man named Oliver Bolton?" Tassie asked.

Annette thought a moment. "I don't think so. Isn't he the man they found buried in Conrad's backyard?"

"Yes," Tassie said. "Do you think it's possible that Conrad murdered him?"

"Conrad?" Annette stared at her. "No. The Conrad I knew could never kill anyone. At least, I don't think he could."

Considering she and Conrad didn't see all that much of each other when they were dating, it wasn't a stretch to assume that Annette didn't know the man as well as she might think.

"Do the police believe Conrad murdered that man?" Annette asked, looking back and forth between her and Jack.

"We're still trying to ascertain that," he said.

The woman nodded but didn't say anything. She definitely seemed unsettled about the possibility though.

Jack took out his card and handed it to Annette. "If you think of anything else, don't hesitate to call."

"I will," she said.

Thanking Annette for her time, Jack stood. Tassie did the same, both of them following Annette to the door.

"Well, everything she said was true," Tassie said when they got to his SUV.

Jack gave her a quizzical look. "How can you be sure?"

"Because Baxter can tell when someone is lying."

His gaze went from her to Baxter and back to her again. "How does he do that?"

She regarded her fur baby thoughtfully then shrugged. "I'm not sure. Maybe he can hear it in their voice or see it in their eyes."

Mouth twitching, Jack reached out to pet Baxter where he was chilling in her arms, his expression skeptical.

"You think I'm imagining it, don't you?" Tassie asked.

She wasn't upset or defensive about it. If she hadn't seen Baxter do his best impression of a lie detector with her own eyes, she might be a little dubious too.

"I know dogs are smart, but…"

"I'll prove it to you," she said.

"And how are you going to do that?"

"With a game of two truths and a lie."

Jack chuckled, clearly amused by that idea.

"Go ahead," she prompted. "Baxter will let me know which is which."

He shook his head with another laugh. "Okay. I'll play along. I was on the lacrosse team in high school. My father is an electrician. And my favorite color is blue."

Tassie grinned. "Your father isn't an electrician."

That proclamation seemed to put him off balance. Jack frowned. "No, he isn't. He's a mechanical engineer. But how did Baxter know that?"

"When someone is lying, he gives me a sideways look," she explained, booping Baxter's nose with hers. "It's his other superpower besides being irresistibly cute."

"That's amazing," Jack said, petting Baxter. "Maybe I should have him in the interrogation room with me when I'm talking to a suspect."

She laughed. "I don't think I want everyone knowing about what Baxter can do or no one will want to talk to me. And that could be an issue if I need to help you on another case. Speaking of which, I was hoping Annette could tell us something more definitive to implicate David. Instead, she told us what we already knew."

"Yeah. Me, too. But murder investigations are never that easy." He took out his keys and pressed the button on the fob to unlock his SUV. "Maybe we'll get lucky and there'll be something incriminating at David's cabin."

Tassie hoped so. But that evidence would only be there if David and Conrad got into the scuffle Allen seemed to think they did.

Chapter 20

As they drove toward Waverly Lake, which was about twenty minutes inland from Bluewater Bay, Tassie had to admit that the water and surrounding area were beautiful if a little too outdoorsy for her liking. She preferred ocean life to lake life, along with sidewalks and...well...indoor plumbing. But to each his—and her—own, she supposed.

Luckily, Jack had been able to get a location for the cabin before they'd left the police station, so they wouldn't have to hike through the woods hoping they'd find it. More importantly, the cabin was close to the lake so no hiking through nature.

As far as Tassie was concerned, that was a win-win.

"We can't go inside without a warrant," Jack reminded her for what seemed like the twentieth time, slowing his SUV to a stop in front of the cabin. "We're only going to look around and see what we can through the windows."

Tassie didn't say anything as she stepped out of the SUV. Maybe he thought she expected them to break into the cabin. She knew better than to do that with a cop around. Not that she made a habit of breaking and entering, of course. She wasn't even sure she'd know how to do it.

It would have made things a lot simpler if David happened to be at his cabin today. Then they probably could have talked him into letting them inside without a warrant. Jack might even have been able to question him. But unfortunately, David was nowhere to be found and the cabin looked like it was locked up tight.

Like back at Annette's place, Tassie held Baxter instead of using the leash. There was no way she wanted him walking around here with his little feet. He could step in poison ivy or something else equally icky.

"So, you were on the lacrosse team in high school, huh?" Tassie asked as they walked toward the small cabin. It looked like it was made of Lincoln Logs, right down to the dark green roof. Only without that distinct Lincoln Log smell. "Were you guys any good?"

"Two-time state champs," he said, glancing around the area as he fell into step beside her.

"Nice. What position did you play?"

"Goalie."

"That's impressive. I heard that's the hardest position to play."

He looked a little surprised. "You're familiar with lacrosse?"

She threw him a grin. "My boyfriend in high school was on the team."

Only he hadn't been good enough to play goalie. And her high school had never gone to the championships either. She'd still enjoyed going to the games with her friends and cheering the team on anyway.

She glanced at Jack, thinking he looked like he could still play. In fact, she'd very much like to watch that.

Smiling to herself at that image, Tassie stepped onto the wooden porch and peeked into the small window beside the door. From where he sat in her arms, Baxter pressed his nose to the glass so he could see too.

The inside of the cabin was as rustic and uncomfortable looking as she imagined. The walls were wood, as were the floors. A simple table with two chairs occupied one side of the room while a pot-belly stove sat across from it against the opposite wall. Unfortunately, there were no signs of a fight or a struggle that she could see.

It seemed like there was another room in the back of the cabin, so maybe there'd be something more helpful there.

On the other side of the door where he was standing looking through another window, Jack appeared to be thinking the same thing.

"Let's take a look around back," he said.

Tassie followed him in that direction as he led the way, glad she'd decided to wear platform lug sole boots with her jeans today as they made their way over the rough ground around a tall stack of firewood several feet from the structure. In her arms, Baxter snapped his head around, his attention fixed on something in the woods surrounding the cabin. A shiver ran down her back as she looked in that direction. But much like last night when Baxter had been on high alert, she didn't see anything.

She quickened her steps to catch up with Jack.

"Everything okay?" he asked, glancing at her.

"Yeah. I think Baxter saw something out there."

Jack looked that way. "Probably an animal."

Tassie hoped it wasn't a bear. Not that she didn't like bears, but she'd prefer not to run into one out here.

If it *was* a bear—or any other animal—nothing came charging out at them as they walked around to the backside of the cabin.

The windows here were a little dirtier than the ones in the front, but they could still see through them well enough. All she saw, though, was a narrow bed, a nightstand, and no sign of a scuffle anywhere.

"Well, this turned out to be a waste of time," she muttered.

Beside her, Jack grunted in what sounded like agreement.

She turned to him, frustration making her want to scream. "What if we can't find evidence linking David to Conrad's murder?"

He cupped her shoulders in his hands, gazing down at her. "We will."

She wasn't so sure.

"We won't let Sara go to jail," he said firmly.

Tassie nodded. She didn't know why but she believed him.

"Come on," he said. "Let's go back to town."

They both turned to head that way but before she could take more than a few steps, a gunshot rang out and something slammed into the cabin right near her head, sending chips of wood flying.

Tassie screamed and hugged Baxter tighter, instinctively shielding him from any danger.

The next thing she knew, Jack was shoving both of them to the ground behind the stack of firewood they'd walked past earlier just as another gunshot echoed in the air.

"Someone is shooting at us!" she said, realizing even as she spoke that she was pointing out the obvious.

Jack took his gun from the holster on his hip. "Yeah, I know."

"Baxter's shaking," Tassie said, cuddling him close as he trembled against her.

"So are you," Jack said.

That's when she realized his free arm was still around her.

"I've never been shot at before," she told him.

"I would hope not."

A third gunshot split the air. This one sounded like it hit the logs stacked in front of their hiding place and she flinched.

"What are we going to do?" she asked.

From where he crouched down beside her, Jack looked from her toward the front of the cabin then back to her.

"You and Baxter are going to run to the SUV while I cover you," he said, taking out his keys and pressing them into her hand. "Then you can pull around and I'll jump in."

Whatever Tassie expected him to say, it wasn't that. Huddled close to her, Baxter seemed just as surprised. She stared at the keys in her hand, then looked at Jack.

"Wait. What?!"

Whoever was out there in the woods shooting at them did it again, hitting the woodpile.

"I can't do that!" she protested.

"Yes, you can," he said, his voice calm and almost infuriatingly reassuring. "Whoever is out there won't be shooting at you because I'll be shooting at him, so he'll be too busy ducking. You and Baxter got this, Tassie. Trust me."

She wanted to, but at the same time, she kept reminding herself that she wasn't some action hero. She was a woman who owned a doggy bakery who was trying to keep a friend out of jail. But Jack was a cop who had way more experience with going up against bad guys than she did. If he thought that their best chance of making it out of this was her and Baxter running to the SUV, then she supposed that's what she and Baxter were going to do.

"Okay," she finally said. "But you'd better be ready to jump in the SUV when I pull around."

"I will be," he promised.

Tassie gazed down at her fur baby. "Okay, Baxter. Let's do this."

Resisting the crazy urge to kiss Jack, Tassie jumped to her feet at the same time as he started shooting in the direction of whoever was out there trying to kill them. She ran as fast as she could toward the SUV, holding Baxter close and shielding him with her body.

Tassie expected to get hit with a bullet any moment, but Jack had been right. The person trying to kill them was more interested in avoiding getting shot himself right now than shooting at her.

Hand shaking, she raced around the SUV, opened the door, and climbed in. Keeping Baxter in her lap, she started the SUV, then put it in gear and spun the vehicle around, heading in Jack's direction.

He was still crouched behind the stack of wood, firing in the bad guy's direction. When he saw her, he sprinted for the SUV while still shooting with one hand. The moment he jumped in, she floored it, fishtailing a little as she sped toward the main road that would take them back to town.

They barely went a mile before Tassie stopped right in the middle of the road. She sat there gripping the wheel with shaking hands, heart hammering in her chest.

"You okay?" Jack asked.

She nodded. "Just a little shaken up." Okay, a *lot* shaken up. "Can you drive so I can hold Baxter?"

Normally, she'd want her pup in his carrier, but right now, he looked like he could use a cuddle. And if she was being honest, so could she.

"Yeah," Jack said, opening the door.

While he strode around to take the wheel, Tassie gently moved Baxter to the seat, then climbed over the center console to sit on the passenger side. Baxter nimbly jumped onto her lap as Jack slid into the driver's seat. She wrapped her arms around her fur baby and let out a sigh of relief as they started down the road again, beyond grateful he hadn't been hurt.

"You did good back there," Jack said, glancing at her. "Both of you."

"Thanks." Tassie caressed Baxter's ears. "Does this kind of thing happen to you a lot?"

He let out a snort. "Getting shot at? No. But someone definitely didn't want us snooping around that cabin."

That was true enough. Though how that someone would explain two dead bodies outside the cabin was anyone's guess. Perhaps they hadn't thought that part through.

"I think we can now safely say that David is the killer," she said.

Because who else could it be?

Chapter 21

Jack called the station on the way back to Bluewater Bay to get officers out looking for David. Because searching the woods would probably be a waste of time since he almost certainly hightailed it out of there, they were checking his home and the usual places he frequented, starting with his charter fishing business.

"You don't think he left town already, do you?" Tassie asked worriedly.

While she was concerned about David coming after her—and Jack—again, she was also nervous about what that could mean for Sara. They couldn't convince anyone she didn't murder Conrad unless they proved David did.

"I don't think so," Jack said with a shake of his head. "There's nothing to make him think we recognized him out in those woods. More likely, he'll keep doing what he's been doing, hanging around town and acting like he's innocent. Which makes me wonder why he tried to kill us today."

Tassie had been wondering that too. Unless there was something incriminating in the cabin that directly tied him to Conrad's murder, it didn't make sense.

"Maybe he panicked?" she suggested.

"Maybe," Jack agreed.

Chief Pennington was waiting for them when they arrived at the police station. Well, actually, he was waiting for Jack. Tassie wasn't even sure the man noticed she was there. That was fine with her. Hugh Pennington was nice enough, but she'd prefer not to have to answer all sorts of questions about why she was snooping around Conrad's cabin. She doubted he'd take kindly to an amateur detective poking her nose into a murder investigation.

Not every cop was as understanding as Jack.

"Why don't you and Baxter go ahead and wait in my office while I talk to the chief," Jack said to her softly.

She nodded. "Okay."

Tassie sure as heck wasn't going to argue. In all honesty, she didn't feel safe wandering around town with David out there. She wasn't sure how the man had known they'd be at his cabin unless he'd been following her since she'd stopped by For Reel Sportfishing. That was a creepy thought.

Had he seen her talking to Allen earlier? If he had, then Allen could be in danger too. She hated to think of something happening to the poor guy because he'd tried to help her.

Unfortunately, Jack was already in Chief Pennington's office giving him a rundown on what had happened at the cabin, so she'd have to wait until he was finished to tell him about Allen. Too bad she hadn't thought to get his phone number when he asked her out for coffee. Then she could have checked on him herself. But she supposed that would have been weird. Especially since she wasn't going to accept his invitation.

Sighing, she and Baxter walked into Jack's office. His desk—which was amazingly tidy—was situated in front of the window so he could sit facing the door while he typed on his computer or did paperwork. Tassie ignored the two chairs in front of the desk and, instead, walked over to look at the framed awards and commendations on the wall near the filing cabinet while Baxter sniffed around, exploring every nook and cranny. Along with the letters of commendation—there were quite a few—there was also a Prestigious Service Medal, a Mayor's Achievement Medal, and a Medal for Bravery from back in Albany.

Considering how he'd saved her life and Baxter's today, Tassie could definitely see how he'd gotten that last one.

Hmm. She wondered if civilians could nominate awards like that in Bluewater Bay.

Did the Bluewater Bay Police Department even give out awards? She'd have to remember to ask Lucy.

Tassie turned to check what Baxter was doing and saw him standing over by the window, pushing the horizontal blinds aside with his nose so he could see outside. He liked to do the same thing at home. It always made her smile. He'd totally cornered the market on cuteness.

She reached into her purse for her phone, figuring she'd scroll through Instagram while she waited for Jack, but it rang the moment she picked it up. She glanced at the screen to see Lucy Face Timing her. Tassie swiped the green button to answer.

"Hey!" Tassie said.

"Hey yourself!" Lucy was leaning back on her couch in the living room on a stack of pillows, hair up in a ponytail. "I just heard on my scanner that the cops are looking for David Campbell."

"You listen to your police scanner on your day off?"

"The baby likes it," she said with a shrug. "But back to David Campbell. They think he murdered Conrad."

Tassie nodded. "I know."

"You do?" Lucy pulled the phone closer, scrutinizing the collection of frames on the wall behind Tassie. After a moment, recognition dawned on her face. "Wait a minute. Are you in Jack's office?"

"Yeah. Jack came with Baxter and me to Cutler's Cove to talk to Conrad's ex-girlfriend. Then we stopped at David's cabin by Waverly Lake on the way back because we thought there might be something there to tie David to Conrad's murder. Long story short, someone started shooting at us."

Lucy's eyes went wide. "What?! Oh, my gosh! Are you and Baxter okay?"

"Yeah, we're both fine." Tassie smiled. "Thanks to Jack."

He honestly *had* been amazing back at the cabin. She still didn't know how he'd stayed so cool, calm, and collected when they'd been getting shot at. She didn't know what she would have done if she and Baxter had gone up there by themselves.

They'd both probably be dead right now.

She shuddered, not even wanting to think about that.

"Are you at the station to give your statement or...? Lucy asked.

Tassie gave herself a mental shake, refusing to think any more about how differently things could have gone at the cabin if Jack hadn't been with them.

"Jack wanted us to wait here while he talked to Chief Pennington," she said. "I think he's worried about David coming after us. I have to admit, I'll feel better when the cops arrest him."

"Me, too."

"Speaking of which, I need to call Abby and let her know what's going on," Tassie said. "Isaac is at the shop with her, but I want them to keep an eye out for David in case he comes looking for me there."

"Good idea. Just promise me that you'll stay with Jack until they catch David, okay?"

"I will," Tassie assured her.

After hanging up, she called her sister to fill her in on what had happened at the cabin. Abby was as worried as Lucy and was relieved she and Baxter were sticking close to Jack until they found David.

"You and Isaac be careful too," Tassie said just as Jack strode into his office. "Jack just walked in. I'll call you later."

She dropped her phone into her purse and gave him an expectant look. "Anything?"

Flashing her a grin, he bent to pet Baxter, who had immediately pranced over to greet him, tail wagging. "A couple of officers picked up David a few minutes ago. They're bringing him in now."

Relief coursed through her. "That's great!"

Jack straightened. "We still have to place him at the cabin and find something to tie him to Conrad's murder but we're that much closer to clearing Sara's name."

Tassie felt another surge of relief at that. "I'm going to go give Sara the good news. Come on, Baxter." She smiled at Jack. "Thank you."

"I couldn't have done it without your help."

"Maybe. But don't worry. I won't tell the chief," she teased.

Jack chuckled. "I'll call you later."

"I'd like that."

Chapter 22

It didn't occur to Tassie that Sara might not be home until she pulled into the parking lot of her apartment building. She let out a sigh of relief when she saw her friend's car parked in its assigned space. Collecting Baxter from his carrier, she went inside and hurried up the stairs to Sara's place.

When it took a little while for her friend to answer, Tassie wondered if maybe she wasn't home after all but then heard voices inside. A moment later, Sara opened the door.

"Tassie!" she said. "Come in."

As she walked into the apartment, Tassie caught sight of Tristan in the kitchen. He was at the stove stirring something in a skillet, Roxie at his feet watching his every move. He glanced over his shoulder at Tassie.

"Hey," he said, giving her a grin.

She waved, returning his smile as she unclipped the leash from Baxter's harness so he could visit with Roxie. Whatever Tristan was cooking for dinner, it smelled delicious. It also reminded her that she hadn't eaten anything since the mini cupcake she'd gotten that morning at Gwen's.

Behind her, Sara closed the door before leading the way into the kitchen. "Do you want something to drink?"

Actually, she was kinda thirsty. "A bottle of water would be great if you have it."

Sara opened the fridge to take one out, handing it to her. "So, what's up? You didn't change your mind about the teddy bear soaps, did you?"

"No! Not at all," Tassie said. "I'm here because I have good news! The police just arrested Conrad's business partner for his murder a little while ago."

Both Sara and Tristan stared at her in surprise, like they weren't sure they'd heard right.

Tristan stopped stirring, hope in his eyes. "Seriously?"

Tassie nodded, giving them a smile. "Yup. I was at the police station with Jack—Detective Sterling—when they picked David up."

Sara glanced at Tristan before turning back to Tassie. "Does that mean I'm not a suspect anymore?"

"According to Jack, this all but clears your name," Tassie told her, still grinning. "The lawyers probably still have to do official paperwork to drop the charges against you though."

Sara squealed and hugged Tristan. Tassie laughed as he spun her about right there in the kitchen, Roxie dancing excitedly around them.

"This means we have two things to celebrate now!" Sara exclaimed when Tristan set her down on her feet again. "An A&R rep from a record label is coming to listen to Tristan's band play this weekend!"

"That's fantastic! Congratulations!" Tassie said, then added, "Although, I'm not sure what an A&R rep does exactly."

Sara laughed. "I didn't know what they did either until Tristan told me. An A&R representative is from the artists and repertoire division of a record label. They find new bands for them to sign."

"Oh!" Tassie said. "Then congratulations are definitely in order."

Tristan gave her a smile that was almost embarrassed. "Thanks. Don't tell anyone but I think my mom had something to do with getting the guy to come to town. I overheard her talking on the phone to someone a couple weeks ago about our band. Since she told the person on the phone she didn't want anyone knowing what she was doing, I didn't let on I heard."

Sara leaned in to kiss his cheek. "It doesn't matter what brought the guy here because once he hears your band he's going to sign you to a record deal on the spot!"

Well, now Belinda's phone conversation Tassie had overheard at the art gallery made way more sense. She'd been talking to someone from a record label, not a hitman.

"So, what made the cops finally look at my old man's business partner?" Tristan asked, glancing at her as he gave the chicken and pasta in the skillet a stir.

Tassie took a sip of water. "A guy who works at the fishing charter said that after Conrad won the lottery, he and David fought all the time. Apparently, Conrad wanted to dissolve their partnership and David wasn't having any of it. A few days before the murder, the two of them got into a huge fight in David's cabin up at Waverly Lake, and when Jack and I went to check it out, someone shot at us. It had to be David."

Sara exchanged startled looks with Tristan.

"Thank goodness you're okay," she said, then frowned. "Wait. Why were you at the cabin with Detective Sterling?"

Tassie gave her a sheepish look. "Remember when I told you Baxter and I have sort of been doing some investigating of our own to help clear your name? Well, this is some of what we've been doing."

Sara appeared equally stunned at that. Her eyes misted with tears, and she rushed over to wrap her arms around Tassie, hugging her tightly. "I know you said you were helping the police, but... Thank you. Thank you. Thank you." She pulled away to smile at Baxter who was standing beside Roxie. "You too, Baxter."

Tassie smiled. "It was the least we could do. Hopefully, David will confess to the murder. Otherwise, Jack will have to find evidence to link him to the crime." Considering they hadn't been able to do it before, that could prove difficult. But she didn't want to mention that to Sara. "Are you sure you didn't see anyone else in Conrad's house that day you fought with him? Because if Conrad's neighbor didn't see anyone else go inside besides you, that means David must have already been there.

Sara shook her head. "I didn't see anyone. But I suppose they could have been in another room, or even upstairs. I didn't look around. I was too focused on telling Conrad off."

Tassie leaned back against the counter with a sigh. "I wish there was some way I could get into Conrad's house to look around."

She could ask Jack but since it was probably still considered a crime scene, he might not be thrilled with the idea.

"Didn't the cops already do that?" Sara asked.

"Probably not. A witness saw you leaving the house and your fingerprints were on the murder weapon. There'd be no reason for them to search it. Even if they did, maybe Baxter and I could pick up something they missed."

Tristan placed a lid on the skillet then turned to look at her. "You know, my old man left everything to me, including the house, so I have a key if you want to go over there and look around."

Tassie pushed away from the counter. "Um, yeah. If you're cool with that."

"If there's something that gets them to drop the charges against Sara, I'm definitely cool with it."

He walked into the entryway to take a set of keys out of the small wicker basket on top of it, then came back and handed them to her.

"One key opens the front door and the other opens the back but I'm not sure which is which," he said apologetically.

"No worries. I'll figure it out," she said. "I'll text if I find anything."

Because if there was anything there to find, she'd find it.

Even if it took all night.

Chapter 23

"On second thought, let's hope this doesn't take all night because I don't feel like hanging around a house after dark where not one but two people were murdered," Tassie said to Baxter as she unlocked the front door of Conrad's house, absently noting that the crime-scene tape was gone. The sun was already low on the horizon as it was but she didn't want to wait until morning to do this. She wanted to make sure this investigation was wrapped up in a nice pretty bow before then. "What about you?"

Beside Tassie, Baxter gazed up at her in agreement.

"Okay," she said. "Let's do this."

Taking a deep breath, she pushed open the door and led the way inside, then closed it behind them. There was a light switch to her left and she quickly flipped it on. A bright glow from overhead bathed the entryway.

The last time she was here, Conrad's body was stretched out on this same floor, that heavy model wooden ship beside him. She'd be lying if she said she wasn't a little creeped out.

But Sara was depending on her. The faster they searched, the faster she and Baxter could get out of here.

"So where should we start?" she asked Baxter.

He looked around as if trying to decide before gazing up at her again.

"A home office—if Conrad had one," she said. "Good idea. I was thinking that too."

Tassie made her way through the house with Baxter one room at a time, turning on lights as they looked for the aforementioned home office. The more she saw of the place, the more she realized it was like one of those popular internet memes come to life.

Tell me you like fishing without telling me.

Because the living room, dining room, kitchen, and even the bathroom all had something related to fishing. From a largemouth bass sculpture to a ship's wheel to a lamp made out of an antique boat motor to a mirror with carved rainbow trout on the frame, this house had it. Conrad had seriously liked fishing.

"Conrad would hate that we're in here," Tassie said as she tried to find that one junk drawer everyone had in their kitchen. "You know that, right?"

Baxter grinned up at her.

She couldn't help smiling too. "I don't know if Tristan is going to sell the place or not, but if he does, hopefully, the people who buy it have dogs and cats and lots of kids. Not because Conrad would absolutely loathe it—well, maybe a little—but because a house deserves a nice family."

When she finally found the junk drawer, it was surprisingly non-remarkable and filled with nothing but take-out menus from various restaurants in town. That would explain why there was very little in the way of cookware in the cabinets she looked in. Now that she thought about it, she realized that it didn't appear as if Conrad used the kitchen very much at all.

"Well, the kitchen is a bust. Let's check out the living room."

Unfortunately, just expensive looking but rather uninviting leather couches and surprisingly modest TV, nothing to place David in the house.

"Not that I know what we're even looking for," Tassie muttered as she guided Baxter into the entryway and headed upstairs.

Why couldn't David have dropped his wallet when he'd killed Conrad?

Then again, if he had, the police would have found it and placed him at the scene. No, what she was looking for would have to be more subtle than that.

Like downstairs, the upstairs was all hardwood floors. So were the steps. Since they were way too slick for Baxter to tackle with his little feet, she carried him to the second floor then set him down when they got to the top.

The first room they came to was a guest bedroom. Simply decorated with the requisite maritime and fishing accents, it looked like it hadn't been used in a long time—if ever. Thinking there probably wouldn't be anything of interest in that room, she led Baxter past it to the next one.

Which was a home office.

Bingo!

Tassie ignored the low bookcases on either wall that seemed to be filled with self-help books and went directly to the desk by the window. She shook her head when she saw that it overlooked the front part of the property. Probably so Conrad could make sure no one was getting too close to his precious lawn.

Pulling out the chair, she sat down.

In addition to a laptop, there was a desk calendar and a few stacks of papers. She checked the calendar to see if Conrad had written anything in the square for the date he'd been murdered. Like who he might have met with. But there wasn't anything. Actually, he hadn't written much on the calendar at all, which made her wonder why he had it in the first place. Didn't everyone use the calendar on their phone or computer anyway?

She shifted her focus to the first stack of papers on the desk. They turned out to be from Conrad's lawyer about dissolving his business partnership with David. While that meant David could have had motive, it didn't prove he murdered Conrad. The next stack was various things Conrad had printed off the internet about different deep sea fishing boats. Maybe they were for the business he'd intended to start?

Again, not much help.

Sighing, she opened the laptop. And found herself staring at a blinking cursor.

"Of course, it's password protected," she muttered.

Tassie flopped back in the chair, then immediately sat up again as a thought occurred to her.

Maybe Conrad wrote his passwords down somewhere. She kept all of hers in a small spiral notebook. Maybe he'd done the same.

She opened the top drawer on the left and riffled through it but didn't find anything except pens, scotch tape, a stapler—and *more* scotch tape. The drawer underneath only had a ream of printer paper, so it didn't take long to look through there either.

Swiveling the chair to the right, she slid open the top drawer and did a double take at the old photo of a couple and a little boy staring back at her.

She'd seen the photo before.

On Oliver Bolton's Facebook page.

It was a picture of him with his parents.

Tassie held it up to show Baxter. "Why would Conrad have a picture of Oliver and his parents?"

Baxter tilted his head a little as he studied the photo. While he did, she noticed the writing on the back.

Mom and Dad's Anniversary.

02/28/1964

Still holding onto the photo, she looked to see what else was in the drawer and was stunned for the second time in as many minutes to find Conrad's Mega Millions winning lottery ticket there.

Even more shocking?

The winning numbers were *1, 2, 4, 6, 9,* and *28.*

What were the odds that the numbers Conrad played just so happened to be the date of Oliver's parents' anniversary?

That was too much of a coincidence.

It also explained how Conrad won the lottery when he never played.

Tassie looked at Baxter. "Well, I think we figured out why Conrad killed Oliver. He murdered his friend and stole his winning lottery ticket."

She tucked the photo and the lottery ticket in her crossbody purse, then quickly looked through the other drawers. Since there wasn't a notebook of passwords anywhere, she decided to forget about the laptop. Unless David had sent threatening emails to Conrad, there probably wouldn't have been much on it to be of any help. Besides, now that Jack had arrested David, they'd most likely get a warrant for the computer.

"Okay, I think we've searched enough in here."

Getting to her feet, Tassie headed for the door, Baxter beside her. Once in the hallway, she stood there for a moment, debating whether to venture into Conrad's bedroom. Part of her thought that might be a step too far, but then the other part reminded her that they were there to get evidence. Still, the thought of searching Conrad's room…

As if impatient for her to decide, Baxter started in that direction, tugging a little on the leash attached to his harness. When she didn't immediately move to follow, he gave her a pointed look over his shoulder.

"You honestly think we should go in there?" she asked.

He gazed at her with a determined expression.

She let out a sigh. "Okay. Lead the way."

Baxter did, making a beeline for the bedroom at the end of the hallway.

The maritime/fishing theme continued in this room too, complete with a huge ship's wheel on the wall above the bed. Besides the closet along one wall, there was a low dresser and two night tables. She eyed the latter.

Did she truly want to look in those?

There could be things in them that she couldn't unsee.

But there could also be something to help Jack charge David with murder.

Drats.

Tassie took a deep breath and walked over to the night table closest to her. Bracing herself, she reached for the knob when Baxter let out a little bark. She glanced over to see him focused on the closet door, ears and tail on full alert.

"Do you want to look in there?" she asked.

He glanced at her, then back at the closet door.

She supposed the night tables could wait.

"Okay, let's see what's in there that's so interesting," Tassie said, letting him lead her across the room.

Reaching out, she slid the door open, revealing a rack full of unremarkable neutral color shirts on the top and a rack of equally conservative pants on the bottom. Nothing to see here. Unless there was a hidden safe behind the clothes.

Baxter yipped, interrupting her thoughts.

Tassie glanced at her precious pup fixated on the row of boots and shoes on the floor of the closet. She crouched down beside him.

"What is it, baby?"

He touched his nose to a pair of boots beside a pair of deck shoes.

She frowned. There didn't seem to be anything special about them.

Baxter nosed them again then tilted his head to look at her. Since he was so insistent, maybe she should take a closer look.

She leaned in so she could inspect them better. That's when she realized the pair of boots seemed to be bigger than the shoes beside it, as well as all of the other footwear in the closet.

That was weird.

Tassie reached out and picked them up. They weren't merely a little bigger than the other shoes and boots in the closet. They were *way* bigger. Conrad had been five-nine at the most. These boots belonged to someone much taller. Someone well over six feet. Someone closer to seven feet in fact.

Someone like...

Baxter booped her hand with his nose to get her attention then turned to look at something on the floor. She lifted the boots she held higher and out of the way to see a dark red stain on the wood floor where they'd been sitting.

Blood.

David didn't murder Conrad.

Allen did.

Suddenly, everything fell into place.

Allen highlighting the feud between David and Conrad.

Allen just happening to bump into her outside the bakery and tell her about a supposed fight at the cabin.

Allen shooting at her, Baxter, and Jack.

The only thing she didn't know was why Allen had killed Conrad. It couldn't have been for the lottery money because Allen had to have known Conrad would leave everything to Tristan.

Setting the boots on the floor, she pressed a kiss to Baxter's head and caressed his ears. "Good job finding these. Let's call Jack and tell him what we found."

Taking her cell out of her purse, Tassie opened up her favorites in her contacts—What? Of course, she'd already added him in there—and clicked on his name. Hopefully, it wouldn't go to voicemail.

"Tassie, what's up?"

"Hey, Jack. I'm in Conrad's house—"

A loud groan on the other end of the phone interrupted her. "Please tell me that you didn't break in."

"Of course not! Conrad left the house to his son. Tristan gave me the key."

"Oh. Okay then," he said, sounding genuinely relieved. "Wait a minute. Why are you at Conrad's house?"

"I was hoping to find something to prove David was here when Conrad was murdered."

"Did you?"

"Not exactly. Because David didn't kill Conrad."

Jack didn't say anything for a minute. "How do you know that?"

"Because Baxter and I found—"

Beside her, Baxter tensed, his hackles suddenly going up at the same time he turned toward the door and let out a sharp bark.

Phone still to her ear, Tassie turned to see Allen standing there, the gun in his hand pointed directly at her.

Chapter 24

Her stomach lurched.

"Tassie, what's going on?" Jack demanded in her ear.

Allen is here and he's going to kill me because I figured out he murdered Conrad.

But she couldn't say that, of course.

"Allen," she said, knowing Jack was listening. "This isn't because I didn't have coffee with you, is it? If it is, we can go get some right now. The gun isn't necessary."

"Don't play dumb," Allen snapped. "Hang up the phone."

She hesitated, hand tightening around her cell.

"I'm on my way," Jack said. "Keep him talking."

"Hang up!" Allen ordered. "Now!"

"Okay, okay."

Pretending to thumb the red button, she slipped the phone in her purse, hoping Jack could still hear what they were saying while it was in there. Quickly bending to pick up Baxter, she cuddled him close as she faced off with Allen.

"Why did you kill Conrad?" she asked.

His mouth tightened like he was afraid to confess. Which was pretty dopey considering he was holding her and Baxter at gunpoint.

"You're going to kill me anyway," she pointed out as casually as she could manage. It took everything in her to act nonchalant when she was staring at certain death here. "The least you can do is satisfy my curiosity."

Allen seemed to consider that. "Because he wouldn't share the lottery money with me."

"Why would he share the money with you?"

"Because that was the deal we made."

"Maybe you should start at the beginning because I'm obviously missing something. Why would he agree to give you a share of the money he won in the lottery?"

He shifted from foot to foot almost nervously which was making her nervous. Well, *more* nervous.

"Because Conrad didn't play the lottery, that's why!"

Tassie frowned. "I'm confused."

She actually wasn't confused at all, but she needed to keep him talking. And if she was being honest, she wanted to hear more about this deal he and Conrad had.

Allen let out a loud sigh of frustration. "Oliver was the one who played the lottery. The winning ticket was his. If Oliver had given us some of the money like he promised, he'd be alive right now, Conrad would be alive right now, and I wouldn't have to kill you because you stuck your nose where it didn't belong. This is all Oliver's fault!"

So, in Allen's mind, everything was somebody else's fault. Maybe she could use that.

"Well, if Oliver said he would share the money with you, then he should have," she agreed.

"Right? He played those same numbers every week for years. None of us expected him to ever win. And then we're all watching TV downstairs that night and they announce the winners and Oliver tells us that he won," Allen shook his head. "Conrad and I figured we'd each get a third since that seemed fair and all, but then Oliver said he wasn't going to share a dime of that money. That he thought we were only joking when we talked about it."

Yeah, that's because most people *would* be joking if they said something like that.

She didn't dare say that out loud though.

"What happened?" she prompted even as she tried to figure out if she was fast enough to get past Allen and make a run for the door before he could stop her.

Probably not. She'd never been super athletic.

She'd have to keep Allen talking until Jack got here.

"Things got ugly between Conrad and Oliver—I mean *really* ugly—and when Oliver tried to leave, Conrad hit him with that heavy model ship he kept in the entryway. Shocked me, I can tell you. I did not expect that." Allen shrugged. "I wanted to dump Oliver's body in the bay. Everyone knew he loved to fish so it'd look like he fell overboard or something. But Conrad said someone might see us, so he suggested we bury Oliver in the backyard instead since no one ever goes back there but him, then take Oliver's lottery ticket. He even took that photo of Oliver's parents with the date of their anniversary on the back. He was afraid someone would put two and two together and figure out the lottery ticket belonged to Oliver. The only mistake I made was trusting Conrad when he said he'd split the money with me."

It seemed like Allen made a lot more mistakes than that. Like helping Conrad bury a body in the backyard instead of going to the police. But she didn't point out the obvious.

"Conrad kept telling me that he had to wait for his lawyer to do some paperwork before he could give me my share. Like an idiot, I believed him," Allen continued. "Anyway, I had enough of his stalling, so I came to talk to him the other day. That's when he told me that he wasn't going to give me half the money. That he was giving it to his son instead."

"I can see how that would make you mad," she said.

Where was Jack? She couldn't keep Allen talking much longer.

"But then that woman showed up—the one the cops arrested for killing Conrad," he added. "I went into the kitchen to cool off while she and Conrad were fighting about his son, so she never saw me. I figured if I waited until after she left and talked to Conrad after I calmed down, I might be able to get him to change his mind about the money."

"But that didn't happen?"

He shook his head. "Conrad didn't want to hear anything I had to say after she left. All he could talk about was his son and that giving him half of the money was the only way to get back into his life. What about my life? Did he think I wanted to work fishing charters forever? I was so angry I could barely see straight." His mouth curved up at one corner. "It was kind of poetic to murder Conrad with the same model ship he killed Oliver with, don't you think?"

Tassie supposed that was true. But the question seemed like it was rhetorical, so she didn't bother to agree.

"What I don't understand is why you put your boots in Conrad's closet," she said.

"Oh. That." He shrugged. "When I realized I got blood on them, I didn't want to track it through the house to the back door so I hid them in the last place I figured the cops would look."

On some level, that made sense. But why not take the boots off then take them with him and dispose of them someplace else?

She would have asked but he continued.

"I tried to come back a few times to get them but that old woman next door was always outside doing something so I couldn't." His mouth tightened. "Everything would have been so much simpler if I'd been able to kill you up at the cabin. I didn't count on you bringing your cop boyfriend with you."

"He isn't my boyfriend," she said automatically.

Although, she wouldn't mind if they were heading in that direction.

Allen didn't look like he believed her. "You sure about that? Because the two of you seemed pretty close the other night when you left The General Store."

She glared at him. "You were following us?"

"I was following *you*," he corrected. "I didn't like all those questions you were asking and thought you might be trouble. It turns out I was right."

In her arms, Baxter let out a little growl. Tassie caressed his fur, hoping to calm him even though she was far from that way herself, something her baby could almost certainly sense.

"You don't have to kill me," she said when she saw Allen level the gun at her more firmly. "I won't tell anyone what I saw here."

He snorted. "Like I'm supposed to believe that. The first thing you'll do is put it on your podcast."

"I don't have a podcast," she said quickly. "I made that up so I could find out who killed Conrad."

"Why do you care so much who killed him?" Allen demanded.

"Because..."

Tassie hesitated. If she told him the real reason was because the woman arrested for his murder was her friend, Allen would never let her leave here alive. And if there was even the smallest possibility that he might, she couldn't risk it.

His face darkened with rage—and fear. "You know what? It doesn't matter. I just need to make sure you never tell anyone who killed him."

Oh, no. Allen was starting to look a little unhinged.

She couldn't wait for Jack. She needed to get herself and Baxter away from this guy now.

Tassie looked behind Allen, pretending to sag with relief. "Jack! Thank goodness you're here!"

As she'd hoped, Allen quickly spun around, a panicked expression on his face.

Tassie rushed past Allen, giving him a hard shove on the way. He stumbled, catching himself against the wall with his free hand. Tassie kept running, sprinting down the hallway to the staircase. Navigating the slick steps at this speed was probably asking for trouble but she didn't slow.

Behind her, Allen had already gotten his feet under him again and was coming after her and Baxter.

She nearly fell down the bottom half dozen steps, catching herself just in time.

Allen wasn't as lucky, sliding down them and hitting the floor of the entryway hard.

Tassie hurried to the door but before she got halfway there, it opened and Jack burst in, gun drawn. He wrapped his free arm protectively around her, turning slightly to put himself between her and Allen, keeping her and Baxter as far away from the man as possible.

"Drop it!" Jack ordered.

On the floor, Allen glared at them, gun still in his hand.

"Now!" Jack added.

Muttering something under his breath, Allen angrily placed the gun on the floor and held up his hands in surrender.

Jack glanced at the uniformed officer with him and gave him a nod. Henry quickly holstered his gun and hurried over to put Allen in handcuffs. Only after that was done and Henry helped him to his feet did Jack slide his gun in the holster he wore and turn to her.

"Are you and Baxter okay?" he asked, looking her over with concern on his face as he gently cupped her shoulders in his hands.

Tassie nodded, her breathing and heartbeat finally slowing to normal. "We are now. That's the second time you saved our lives today."

He gave her a lopsided grin. "Just doing my job. I'm only glad I got here in time."

She returned his smile. "Me, too. Thank you."

Before either of them could say anything else, Baxter leaned forward to lick Jack's face, then grinned. Tassie and Jack both laughed. That's when she realized how close Jack was standing.

Gaze holding hers, he slowly lowered his head to kiss her, and her pulse sped up again, for a different reason altogether this time.

"Detective."

She and Jack immediately stepped away from each other at the sound of Henry's voice. Tassie felt herself blush as Jack cleared his throat.

"What is it, Henry?" he asked.

To his credit, Henry didn't act as if he'd interrupted anything. Or maybe he didn't know?

"Just wanted to let you know that we're going to bring the suspect to the station for booking," he said.

Jack nodded, glancing at her out of the corner of his eye. "That's fine. I'll be down there in a few minutes."

Henry gave them both a nod, then disappeared outside. Jack looked at her, his gaze lingering on her lips for a moment. "Um... The chief is going to want a statement from you."

"Okay. I'll follow you to the station then." She reached into the purse for the keys Tristan had given her. "You'll need these. There's a pair of boots in the closet upstairs with blood on them that'll prove Allen murdered Conrad."

Jack took the keys as he closed the door behind them, his fingers brushing hers.

As they walked over to where her SUV was parked, a thought occurred to her and she frowned. "You didn't really think I broke into Conrad's house, did you?"

Chapter 25

"So much for Bluewater Bay being the quiet, little town you thought when you took this job, huh?" Tassie teased. "Although, if it were that quiet, little town, we might not have met."

Jack chuckled. "I don't know. I'd still bring Gus to the dog park or stop by Pupcakes to get him treats. I get the feeling that we would have met anyway."

That was true, she supposed. But would she and Jack have had any reason to hang out together if there hadn't been a murder to solve? Sitting beside him on the bench at the dog park while Baxter and Gus frolicked and played nearby, she decided the answer to that question was yes. Something told her that their pups would have brought them together.

Not that they were *together* together yet. It had only been a week since they'd solved Conrad's murder. But he and Gus had come into Pupcakes a few times already and this was the second time they'd run into each other at the dog park, so things were trending in the right direction.

"Thanks for keeping my name out of things as much as possible," she said. "I'm not sure Chief Pennington would have appreciated my help in the investigation."

She'd been concerned about what to say in her statement so Jack had suggested saying that Tristan had given her the key so she could get an early look at the items that'd be available at the estate sale. She wouldn't be interested in anything in Conrad's home, but the chief didn't know that. As for everything else in the inheritance, because Conrad came by the lottery money illegally, unfortunately, Tristan wasn't entitled to any of it.

"Maybe not," Jack agreed. "But the mayor would have calmed the chief down. Poole couldn't be happier that we solved the case before the TV people get here for that baking competition. He's convinced it'll put Bluewater Bay on the map."

She smiled. "If the mayor said that to me, I would have a hard time resisting the urge to pull up Google Maps on my phone and show him that Bluewater Bay is already on there."

Jack let out a chuckle. "That's why I like you. You're quick on your feet and you make me laugh. Among other things."

Tassie wondered what those other things were, but Baxter and Gus chose that moment to run over for pets and kisses. By the time they went back to playing, Jack had already changed the subject.

"So, what'll you do with all your free time now that there isn't a murder to investigate?"

Was that his subtle way of trying to ask her out?

Or was he waiting for her to make the first move?

"Go back to what I usually do," she said. "Bake doggy treats, run Pupcakes with my sister, and plan Lucy's baby shower."

He flashed her a grin. "Ah. The one where you might need police presence if the cupcakes start flying."

She laughed. "That's the one."

"Well, remember that my offer still stands if you need a cop there."

"I'll keep that in mind."

Tassie watched Baxter and Gus playfully chase each other up and down the agility ramps for a moment before glancing out at the blue water of the bay. It was hard to believe that a couple of weeks ago, not one but two murders had rocked the town. But today, the sun was shining and the weather felt decidedly springlike. In the distance, she could hear the horn of a tugboat and closer, the barks and honks of harbor seals. It was nice to have things back to normal.

"You know, it's quite possible that Bluewater Bay will turn into that quiet, little town again," she said, looking at Jack.

"I don't know about that," he said, a teasing glint in his eye. "I have a feeling that with you, things are always going to be interesting around here."

Something in Jack's voice made Tassie think he was looking forward to that.

And so was she.

Afterword

Tassie and Baxter are back in Cupcakes and Corpses to help their favorite detective investigate the murder of a local celebrity influencer who's killed at a baking competition!

Pupcakes Bakery owner Tassie Drake is ready for life to return to normal--or as normal as possible, given just last month, she and her Chiweenie, Baxter, helped the hunky new town detective, Jack Sterling, solve a murder. But spring is in full bloom, and that means tourist season is too. Adding to the excitement, The Dessert Channel is filming their TV show Cupcake Combat in the park. And Tassie's a firm believer that something sweet can fix just about anything. Except murder.

When one of the cupcake judges drops dead on set, all clues point to murder. But who had the most to gain from the YouTube foodie sensation being killed? Everyone on stage that day is a suspect--two of whom are Tassie's friends. While the last thing Tassie intended to do was get involved in another mystery, spending more time with Jack is icing on the cupcake, especially since their official first date keeps getting interrupted.

But as Tassie and Baxter discover, the dead woman made several enemies on her climb to the top, and someone took sweet revenge. Someone who isn't afraid to kill again…

About the author

Paige is a New York Times and USA Today bestselling author of cozy mystery, romantic suspense, and paranormal romance. She and her very own military hero (also known as her husband!) live on the beautiful Florida coast with their adorable fur baby (also known as their dog!).

You can find Paige's books in eBook and paperback online and at bookstores everywhere.

https://paigetylertheauthor.com/